For more than forty years,
Yearling has been the leading name
in classic and award-winning literature
for young readers.

Yearling books feature children's
favorite authors and characters,
providing dynamic stories of adventure,
humor, history, mystery, and fantasy.

Trust Yearling paperbacks to entertain,
inspire, and promote the love of reading
in all children.

OTHER YEARLING BOOKS YOU WILL ENJOY

NORTH BY NIGHT: A STORY OF THE UNDERGROUND RAILROAD, *Katherine Ayres*

MACARONI BOY, *Katherine Ayres*

STEALING FREEDOM, *Elisa Carbone*

TROUT AND ME, *Susan Shreve*

PICTURES OF HOLLIS WOODS, *Patricia Reilly Giff*

SONG OF SAMPO LAKE, *William Durbin*

DAUGHTER OF MADRUGADA, *Frances M. Wood*

HALFWAY TO THE SKY, *Kimberly Brubaker Bradley*

SILVER DOLLAR GIRL

KATHERINE AYRES

A YEARLING BOOK

Published by Yearling, an imprint of Random House Children's Books
a division of Random House, Inc., New York

ISBN: 0-440-41705-8

Reprinted by arrangement with Delacorte Press

Printed in the United States of America

August 2002

11 10 9 8 7 6

for Becky and Bill,
my ambassadors to the Colorado Rockies

and in loving memory of my great-grandfather
Valentine Carter,
who left home to make his way in the world
at age twelve, in 1898

SILVER DOLLAR GIRL

1

A Heart of Gold

At the landing, halfway up the front stairs, Valentine Harper stopped to study the bright patterns of light spilling onto the window seat from the stained-glass window above. Shifting her schoolbooks from her right arm to her left, she turned and climbed to the second-floor hall. Near the top, she stopped again. Something felt wrong.

Bridget always closed the doors after she straightened the beds, but that afternoon Vallie's bedroom door stood open. Harold must have invaded her room again.

She ran along the hall and charged into her room. The white spring coverlet on the bed lay as crisp and smooth as one of Bridget's aprons. And Harold, sneaky as a weasel, couldn't smooth sheets worth spit, which meant he hadn't put something nasty in her bed again. She dropped to her knees and peered underneath but saw only polished pine floor.

In the clothes cupboard Vallie saw more signs of Bridget's careful work—clean dresses were hanging from their usual pegs and starched petticoats were lined up in a row. Nasty Harold hadn't messed here today either. Once he'd tied her pantalets in knots.

The dresser, washstand, rocking chair and bookshelf all seemed in order and untouched. Then something caught Vallie's eye. One of the curtains that surrounded the window seat was bunched up.

As Vallie stepped closer she noticed strips of shimmery blue cloth and little bunches of white fluff stuck to the green velvet cushion. *Oh, no,* she thought as she shoved aside the curtain. Back in one corner lay a misshapen lump. Vallie's stomach churned. That lump was her doll.

Maria's painted china face still smiled, her bright blue eyes still looked out, but the rest of her! Her dark brown curls had been tugged and mussed. Her blue satin dress had been torn to ribbons, her lace petticoats shredded and her soft cloth body ripped until chunks of cotton stuffing poked out every which way.

Vallie hugged Maria to her chest and squeezed her eyes to hold back the tears. The doll had come in the mail, a gift for her twelfth birthday.

"She reminds me of you, Valentine, with her chocolate brown curls, her blue eyes and her smiling face,"

Papa had written from Colorado. "Something tells me this doll has a heart of gold, just as you do, Dear Daughter. Keep her with you always, your secret strength in times of trouble. Happy Birthday, my sweet."

Vallie sniffed and examined Maria once more. Only the face and hands were undamaged—Harold hadn't smashed the china parts. That didn't make sense.

She turned and studied her perfectly made bed. *Of course,* she thought. Wretched Harold had arranged this to look like the work of Mischief, the kitchen cat, just as he had with his filthy prank two weeks ago.

The memory of that horrible night sent a shudder along her spine. At first, she'd not noticed anything unusual, not until she turned back the coverlet to crawl into bed and found a dead mouse on her pillow. Her scream had brought the entire household running to her room.

Bridget arrived first, her green eyes flashing fire. Then Aunt Margaret, clutching her dressing gown, followed by Uncle Franklin, complaining about losing his night's rest for some flighty female he shouldn't have to worry about. Finally Harold showed up, with a sleepy, innocent look pasted over his face. He'd fooled Aunt Margaret and Uncle Franklin well enough, and poor Mischief had been locked outdoors for three days as punishment. *Not this time.*

Tucking Maria under one arm, Vallie charged across her room and down the hall. Without stopping to knock, she shoved open Harold's door.

"Well, hello, Cousin," Harold said from where he was sprawling comfortably on his bed. "What brings you to my room? Did you want to have a friendly chat?"

"I'd sooner make friends with a copperhead. Why did you rip up my doll?" She shoved Maria right under his freckled nose.

"Me? Whatever gave you the idea that I'd hurt your poor, dear dolly?"

Vallie's hands curled into fists. "You're mean and you're a bully. I'm going to tell your friends on you. I'll tell them how you pick on me—a girl, and a whole year younger. See what they say about that."

"You just try it," he said, glaring. Then he sat up and smiled as if he were the nicest boy around and called out, "Mother. Oh, Mother. I think you'd better come upstairs right away."

"You're not going to blame poor Mischief again. I won't let you."

"You think you can stop me?"

Aunt Margaret stepped into Harold's room with a sheet of notepaper in one hand. "Yes, dear. What is it?" She looked from Harold to Vallie with a half smile on her face.

"Aunt Margaret, my doll—"

Harold interrupted. "That naughty kitchen cat has

hurt poor Cousin Valentine's doll. We really should do something—she's quite mean. And look here." He stuck out one pudgy arm. "She scratched me."

"If Mischief scratched him, she had a reason," Vallie said. "He was—"

"I was trying to rescue your silly doll. That's the reason." While Aunt Margaret bent to examine his arm, he stuck out his tongue at Vallie.

Aunt Margaret sniffed. "Dreadful cat. I'll speak to Bridget right away. Now, have you washed that scratch, Harold? We don't want it to fester."

"Would you please wash it for me, Mother? I'm not so very brave about cuts."

"Well, of course, my sweet boy . . ."

Vallie turned in disgust and marched back to her own room. She shut the door tight and climbed into the window seat with her doll still in her arms. Aunt Margaret was hopeless.

So was Maria. Vallie patted the soft, half-empty body. It would take forever to stitch up every rip, and her fingers were more suited to helping Bridget knead fat loaves of bread than to making tiny stitches. Still, she pinched a wad of cotton between her fingers and poked it into a hole. Something stopped her finger—something hard, right in the middle of Maria's cloth body.

Vallie rolled the doll over and slipped her finger into a long rip on the back. Sure enough, something stiff filled the center.

"Sorry, Maria," Vallie whispered as she reached into the rip and pulled out a handful of stuffing, then another, exposing a packet wrapped in brown paper. Her fingers shook as she tugged at the paper. Finally it came loose, and she eased it out of the limp body and set Maria aside.

The packet weighed heavy in her hand. Someone had tied careful knots. As Vallie unfolded the brown paper, shining round weights dropped into her skirts. Gold! Somebody had filled her doll with five gold eagles, each of them worth ten dollars.

Papa's words came back to her, and she understood. ". . . this doll has a heart of gold . . . your secret strength in times of trouble." He had sent Maria last winter, but for more than company.

The late-May sun set the gold pieces afire. Vallie sat thoughtfully and studied them. She'd done as her father had asked—obeyed Aunt Margaret and Uncle Franklin, studied hard in school, tried not to make extra work for Bridget and gotten along as well as anyone could with that weasel Harold around.

And she'd waited out the year that her father needed to make his fortune in Colorado. Then another four months, almost five, had passed and it was May 1885. Still he hadn't sent for her to join him; his letters spoke of *nearly* and *almost* and *soon.*

"What if this is a sign?" she asked Maria's sweet face. "What if I was supposed to find the gold today, just when Harold was so cruel?"

She hugged Maria tight. "Papa said it himself. You are surely a strength, and if this isn't a time of trouble, I'll eat my shoe." She turned to the window and looked out into the backyard and beyond, to where the sun hung low in the sky, shining gold like one of her eagles. "West," she whispered. "I'll come West to find you, Papa. Just see if I don't."

2

Playing Hooky

A knock came at her bedroom door. Vallie sat straight, slipped the gold pieces into her pocket and tucked Maria and all her tatters behind the green velvet curtain.

"Valentine, girl. Are you there?" Bridget's voice sounded as warm as the sun on Vallie's back.

"Yes. Please come in."

The door opened and Bridget Joyce crossed the room with a small frown on her pale face. "And why are you hiding behind the curtains, girl? Have you done mischief at school, then?"

"I haven't done any wickedness. But Harold has. Look!" Vallie pulled back the curtain.

"What a piece of work he's done." Bridget took up the doll and examined the body, turning it in her large, kind hands.

Vallie ran one finger along Maria's rosy cheek. "He blamed the cat again, Bridget. That's why he didn't break the face or the fingers."

"Aye, but her face and fingers are just fine, aren't they? Besides which, with all your hugs Maria's chemise and pantalets were going a bit gray, weren't they, now? I'll warrant she could use a new set. Why, I've spent so much time turning you and the missus out for the season, I've neglected poor Maria. I'd wager she'll forgive me though."

Vallie took a deep breath. "You . . . you can fix her, Bridget?"

"And who better, girl? You wouldn't trust Maria to the likes of that thick-thumbed Lizzie O'Reilly next door, would you?"

Vallie felt a smile creep over her face. Bridget had taken care of her for as long as she could remember—as nursemaid first, and then as a friend. "She's in the best of hands with you, Bridget. And could you find a place to hide Mischief for a while? You know Aunt Margaret."

"Leave it to me. You'll have your Maria back in no time, better than new." Bridget shook her head. "That missus does have a blind spot when it comes to His Royal Highness, Prince Harold. Should have had six children instead of just the one and he wouldn't be so spoiled."

Bridget's words warmed Vallie's heart. The young

Irish woman had figured Harold out right away. His mother did spoil him. Vallie was an only child too. But Papa was in Denver and hadn't done his share of spoiling this past year. Vallie bit down on her bottom lip.

"Now tidy yourself, girl, and splash a bit of water on your face." Bridget gathered up Maria and all the scraps and bundled them into her apron. "Your friend Jenny Rittenhouse has come to call. Shall I send her up?"

"I really don't feel like—"

"Well, of course you don't," Bridget said, pulling Maria closer. She placed one large, warm hand on Vallie's forehead. "Shall I tell Miss Jenny you've got the sniffles?"

"Isn't that a lie?"

"Is it?" Bridget shook her head. "Here's what I'll say. Miss Valentine's nose is red and she's been sniffling. I'm about to dose her with a hot cup of spearmint tea. Every word is precisely true."

"Thanks, Bridget. Tell Jenny I'll see her tomorrow."

As Bridget shut the door behind her, Vallie stepped closer to the mirror over her washstand and studied her face—the thin cheeks, the blue eyes and the dark shining hair that hung to her waist. That bit of red around her nose would disappear by tomorrow, so no one at school would know about her troubles with Harold.

Vallie wrinkled her nose in the mirror and thought hard. Those sniffles. If she played sick and didn't go to school tomorrow . . . Nobody at home would have to know—Harold went to a boys' school on the far side of Allegheny and he left an hour earlier than she did. At school, Jenny would tell the teacher about the sniffles. Then . . .

Vallie took a deep breath. Her backbone tingled. She felt naughty thinking this way, but surely her thoughts were not as wicked as Harold's evil deeds.

She *could* sneak out to the depot tomorrow, ask questions and see how far her gold eagles might help her fly. But did she dare?

"It's time to see what you're made of," she said, shaking her finger at the Vallie in the mirror. She stuck her hand into her pocket and felt the warm heaviness of the coins. Gold had a way of giving a person courage. She spoke to the mirror again, with a decisive nod. "You're no coward, Valentine Harper. Of course you'll go."

The next morning, Vallie got up and dressed soon after the sun showed. Between fretting about what Harold might do next and hoping she wouldn't get caught playing hooky, she'd slept only in patches. And she'd found herself checking under the pillow through the night for the gold eagles she'd hidden there.

After she buttoned her yellow gingham dress and

laced up her sturdy walking oxfords, she rustled into the back of her clothes cupboard, behind the winter dresses, for a pair of white woolen stockings she had tossed into the bottom. They'd grown too short by Christmas, but after Harold had helped himself to the contents of her tin bank last fall, she'd used them as a hiding place for the spending money Aunt Margaret doled out according to Papa's instructions.

The stockings felt heavy—nickels and dimes had piled up all winter and spring though she'd been careful to drop a few pennies into the tin bank from time to time, to keep Harold from suspecting that she'd been hiding coins.

Two dollars and sixty-five cents, she counted. Not a fortune, like her eagles, but it would help. She scooped the money into the small cloth purse Bridget had sewn to match her dress, added the gold pieces and tied the drawstring tight.

Hiking up her skirts, she untied both of her petticoats, slipped the purse strings over the petticoat laces and retied the laces tightly. As she walked, the purse bumped around. *Good,* Vallie decided. It would keep her from forgetting the seriousness of her task.

She hurried through an early breakfast of oatmeal with Uncle Franklin, who rustled newspapers and mumbled to himself as he ate. Dirty dishes in the kitchen confirmed her hope that Harold had already eaten and left for school. Safe so far. She was letting herself out the front door as Aunt Margaret called out from the steps, "Vallie. Where are you off to so early?"

"I . . . I have to practice my poem for the end-of-year school exercises. It's supposed to be a surprise," Vallie said. "See you this afternoon, ma'am."

"A poem. How nice, dear. Hurry then, be good for your teacher. Make your family proud."

Aunt Margaret's kind words made Vallie's ears burn, but she refused to think about turning back. Instead, she slipped out onto the porch, where the morning air cut right through the yellow gingham dress. She tugged her shawl tight around her shoulders and felt her hidden purse thump against her leg as she hurried down the steps.

Avoiding the sidewalk, she ducked behind the house to Butternut Alley and made tracks for Federal Street and the train depot. As she hurried, the morning chill lifted, and with it her spirits. *I might just get away with this,* she thought, grinning at the notion.

When she reached the wide avenue, she slowed and looked around. People were already out, going about their morning business. If she walked directly to the depot, she'd pass the Market House and the busiest parts of Allegheny City. Surely someone would recognize her, so she crossed over and made her way to the train tracks instead. For as far as she could see, trees and bushes hid the tracks from view; they'd hide her as well.

At first she walked the rails, balancing on the thin strips of metal like a high-wire walker. Then a train whistled in the distance and she jumped down, away from the tracks.

A chuffing sound grew to a loud clacking roar. A locomotive sped away from the depot, spewing dust, soot and cinders into the air. Car after car hurtled along behind. Vallie counted them as they passed. Flatbed cars filled with steel bars flew by, followed by closed boxcars, and cattle cars, which added mooing and animal smells to the morning. As she saw the glimmer of a red caboose, she waited out the freight's passage.

Once the train rounded the bend beyond the park, she climbed back up to the roadbed and walked between the tracks, where ties and cinders made a sturdy path for her oxfords. As she trudged on, large buildings loomed on both sides of the track—the Allegheny Seminary on her right, the Western Penitentiary on the left. Odd, she'd never noticed how close the buildings stood—saints on one side, sinners on the other.

She wasn't acting like a saint today, but she wasn't a true sinner either. Nor a scalawag nor a ruffian. Just a girl who needed her father. Surely they didn't send a person to jail for missing one day of school. Holding tight to the thought of her father, she hurried along until she saw the tall brick depot building with its six columns, curving roof and red chimneys stretching a full three stories high.

It's like a castle, Vallie decided. She straightened her shoulders and tried to look as if she belonged in such a fancy place.

3

The Price of a Ticket

Vallie lifted her chin and strode into the depot as if she knew exactly what she was doing. On all sides travelers rushed toward the tracks, making it hard for her to see where she was going. She walked smack into a porter hauling a cartload of trunks and bumped her shin on a wheel.

"Watch it!" he shouted. "People got trains to catch."

"Sorry."

The porter scowled at her and hurried away. Straight ahead, people waited in a long line at the ticket booth. She stepped into line behind a large man and stared at a pair of moles on the back of his red neck. He shifted his weight from one side to the other and cleared his throat. Then, as if he'd felt her stares, he turned and looked her in the eye.

"Well, now. What's a young miss like yourself doing here today?"

What indeed? Vallie's cheeks grew warm. "I'm doing an errand . . . for my family," she said. "I've a note about it, for my teacher." She patted her dress pocket as if it contained a note.

"Hrmph," the man grumbled.

"Truly," Vallie continued. "I'll hurry to school as soon as I finish." She smiled and tried not to look as if she'd just told a large fib.

"Stop! Stop, thief!"

Vallie spun around in time to see a tall man running after someone. Others joined the chase, including a clean-shaven man who wore a dark uniform. They were heading right for her.

She grabbed for her purse through her skirts and tried to step aside, but the crowd was too thick. A boy bumped into her, then turned and ran for the doorway. The uniformed man grabbed the boy and there was more yelling and thumping.

"Got you! It's off to jail with you, you thieving scoundrel."

As the man towed the thief away, Vallie stood clutching her money and feeling helpless. The thief was just a rough boy, not much older than she was, but if he'd tried to steal her gold, she couldn't have stopped him any more than she'd been able to stop Harold when he wanted to do wickedness.

Vallie swallowed hard. Perhaps this trip wasn't a good idea after all. But she was already at the station, might as well ask questions as she'd planned. It didn't mean she actually had to travel anywhere.

"Dad-blamed wickedness," said the man behind her.

Vallie turned. This man looked kindly enough, with a wrinkled face and gray beard. After a moment, she realized he was talking about the thief, not her. "I was frightened," she admitted.

"And well you should be, a young girl like yourself in a place like this. What's your mother thinking of? Lucky that yard bull was here."

"Yard bull?"

"Railroad police. They watch for thieves in the freight yards and patrol the depots. Sharp they are; not much gets by their notice. Good thing, too, since you were foolish enough to come here alone."

"Um, yes." Vallie swallowed and turned around. Suddenly she felt very foolish indeed and unsafe in the depot. She'd just witnessed a crime. And she hadn't known there were railroad police who noticed everything, including girls who should be in school and weren't. She stepped closer to the man behind her, hoping the yard bulls might think they were traveling together and not discover that she was playing hooky.

At last it was Vallie's turn. She edged forward and smiled at the ticket seller. "I'd like to travel to Denver, please."

"Pardon?"

"Denver. It's in Colorado."

"I know where Denver is, missy. But you wouldn't be traveling there alone, would you? Delicate young girl, wouldn't be safe."

Vallie had almost reached the same conclusion, but hearing the man say it aloud made her stiffen her spine. Who was he to tell her where she could or couldn't travel? She smoothed her skirts and wondered why grown-ups always thought they should tell a young person what to do, even if they were strangers. She wouldn't behave that way when she was grown. She'd assume that a person, even a child, had good reasons for her actions.

She flung her shoulders back, just the way Bridget would when challenged. "Of course I'm not traveling alone," she began.

She needed a traveling companion, and quickly. It should probably be someone older and male. Someone like Harold, but she'd never want to travel with him. She wouldn't even spit out his name here; it would cause bad luck for sure. Whose name could she use?

William Rittenhouse! She'd borrow Jenny's brother. "My brother William and I will be joining our father in Denver for the summer."

"Your brother, huh? And why ain't he here to buy the tickets?"

Vallie took a deep breath before answering. "William, at this very minute, is preparing for his examinations. He attends the University of Pennsylvania in Philadelphia. He asked me to obtain all necessary information so that we may travel west as soon as he arrives in Pittsburgh." Her voice sounded false to her ears, even though parts were true.

"So you'll be wanting two fares then. Parlor car? Pullman? Sleeper?"

So many choices. "Just the prices, please."

"Let's see, here to Chicago, regular coach would be ten-fifty. Add on another five or six dollars for a Pullman fare. Then on to Denver, probably another twenty-five for coach, plus twelve or fifteen for them fancy cars."

Vallie added the numbers. Thirty-five just for coach. *Ouch.*

The man grinned at her, but it wasn't a friendly grin.

She lifted her chin. "And the route. When does the train leave, sir?"

"Seven trains go west every weekday. Course two only go to Ohio. And the Limited Express is all Pullman cars. That leaves four regular trains, a morning, two middays, a night. Here's the timetable."

The man spoke fast and Vallie was sure he was trying to confuse her. She took the timetable and tried to make sense of the tiny printing. "How long does it take to reach Denver, please?" Her voice came out in a squeak.

He shrugged. "Depends. Weather, cows, track repair, lots of things can slow down a train. That happens, you might miss the connecting train in Chicago, or Omaha, say. You and *your brother* could reach Denver in three to five days." He grinned again.

The purse under her skirts seemed to grow lighter as he spoke. Three to five days. Even the cheapest coach ticket cost so much money, and she'd need food, maybe even places to stay. And she'd need even more money to travel from Denver to the mountains.

Vallie ducked from the booth. She felt her courage slipping away fast, and she needed to sit down. Clutching the train timetable, she stepped through a doorway into a squarish room filled with rows of benches. Several women sat, holding babies. Young children bounced on the leather seats or played hide-and-seek between the benches. Off in a corner, Vallie found an empty bench and slumped down to examine the schedule.

Pittsburgh, Allegheny, Bellevue, Emsworth—the list went on and on. She patted her lap and felt the weight of her gold eagles. They'd fly away in no time if she made this trip. Maybe she'd run out of money and get stuck in a strange town, miles from Denver and the mountains.

She looked around the ladies' waiting room. Certainly females could travel by train, but all the females here were grown women or little girls with their mothers. Nowhere in the station had she spotted a girl of her age traveling alone.

She slumped down farther on the bench. A waste of time, that's what today had been, she decided. She'd come all this way to slam into porters, lie to strangers, get bumped by ruffians, and have ticket sellers scowl at her. And those yard bulls. She hadn't tried to lift a man's wallet, but she'd told fibs—lots of them. Railroad police were well trained; they'd sniff out falsehoods fast.

Vallie needed to get herself away from the depot and all the strangers milling about. She made a quick trip to the necessary, then hurried from the ladies' waiting room, crossed the crowded main room and ran outdoors.

From the depot's fancy doorway, she could see South Park and the Market House. Beech Street and Aunt Margaret's lay beyond, but as she turned her feet in that direction, she realized the full cost of her mistake. It was still morning and she couldn't arrive at home until school had let out.

She needed a place to wait out the day. And she had to figure out what she'd do tomorrow, when her teacher asked for a note from Aunt Margaret to explain her absence.

4

The House on Resaca Street

Vallie retraced her steps until she reached the railroad tracks. She walked halfway to Aunt Margaret's house, then stopped to catch her breath in a clump of maple trees and looked about. Not much time had passed—it wasn't nearly time for school to let out.

Early this morning she'd rushed around, only thinking as far as the depot. Now she'd pay for her hurry with a rumbly stomach and a dry mouth. She could walk to the Market House and spend a nickel, but she'd probably run smack into Bridget or Aunt Margaret.

Well, why not go home? she asked herself. Not to Aunt Margaret's house on Beech Street, but to her own, real house. Vallie straightened her shoulders and walked along the railroad ties, wishing for a pail of water. It was warmer now as the sun rose higher, dustier too.

At last she left the tracks and turned toward Resaca Street. The cobbles underfoot gave way to bricks, making the street feel like an old friend.

The steps of number 1212 gleamed white in the noonday sun. The front windows shone as if polished by careful hands. Her father had chosen good tenants whose rent paid for her expenses and Bridget's wages, even if Uncle Franklin was always grumbling about his pocket growing empty when her shoes grew too tight.

Vallie wouldn't knock on the door and try to visit. That wouldn't be polite—and it might get her in trouble if someone knew she wasn't in school. But she could watch the house for a while. Slipping along a side street, she headed for Day Alley. It looked just as it always had, bumpy and dusty, with sheds for horses, traps and equipment.

When she reached the red brick wall behind number 1212 she peered around, gathering her courage. With trembling fingers, she opened the latch and sneaked into the backyard, to her old hiding place between the wall and the shed. What a relief for her tired feet when she sat in the familiar space. She wriggled her toes and looked at the washing hanging from the lines, billowing white sheets and pillowslips, shirts and blouses, tiny clothes too.

A latch clicked and the back door opened, forcing Vallie to scoot deeper into the shadows. She shouldn't be here. Visiting was one thing, spying was another.

A woman carried a wicker basket out the door and off the porch. She bent and lifted something out of the basket. A little boy. He wobbled around in the grass on unsteady legs.

"Good boy, Thomas," the woman said. "Helping Mama with the washing. Here's a peg for you to hold, my big strong man."

The little boy smiled and stuck the wooden peg in his mouth. His mother pulled dry clothing from the line and kept crooning to him in a sweet, soft voice.

Vallie's throat closed up. *What am I doing here? This isn't home anymore.* The little boy flung his clothes peg and gurgled. His mother bent and kissed the top of his fluffy, blond head, then carried him back inside.

Vallie waited until the woman had hauled in her wash basket, then scooted out into the alleyway. She needed to find a better place to hide, even if it was just Aunt Margaret's dusty carriage barn. Still, as she carefully made her way along back alleyways, that little boy stayed in her mind.

Vallie closed her eyes. She imagined herself back, a long time ago, before the bad spring flood and the cholera that came after. She could almost see herself as a little child again, with dark fluffy hair. *Her* beautiful mama carried *her* out to help with the washing. Surely Mama kissed *her* head and talked silly talk to *her*.

Frustrated, Vallie opened her eyes. She couldn't remember Mama—only Papa's face inhabited her memory. And he was so far away, it wasn't fair. She belonged with him, but she'd just wasted a whole day discovering that she couldn't travel to Colorado to find him. *All right then,* she decided. *If I can't go, I'll do the next best thing.*

After spending several hot hours in the carriage barn, she slipped back into Aunt Margaret's house, rinsed her face, sipped some cool water and started a letter—

Dear Papa,

School is nearly done and I'm ready to come and join you. Bridget has stitched my summer clothes and I could pack them in a trunk. Please send for me right away. . . .

By the time Bridget served supper, Vallie had finished her letter, carried it to the post office and stitched up a money belt for her gold pieces so that she could wear her eagles at all times and keep them out of Harold's grubby fingers. After supper, she practiced carefully until she could write a fair copy of Aunt Margaret's name.

Dear Miss Wilson:

Please excuse my niece Valentine Harper who was absent from school yesterday due to indisposition.

Yours most sincerely,
Mrs. Franklin Collinsworth

A forgery. It was a bad thing to do, but in Vallie's mind not nearly as wicked as her cousin's behavior or that pickpocket down at the depot. She could make it through the next few days until the end of school. Then her father would send for her. How hard did a person have to wish to make it come true? she wondered.

That night, Vallie tossed about in her bed. She kept seeing the pickpocket and the man with the moles parading past her old house. She thrashed in the bed, trying to make the faces go away, but all the rolling only made her feel hot, so she threw off her covers. When at last she slept, the same pictures returned as dreams.

Morning dawned gray, and Vallie felt every step of yesterday's long walk as she sat up in bed. She swung her legs to the floor and stood, then stopped. Her head felt odd, light, unbalanced. She reached up with her right hand and felt her neck. There, where one of her braids should be, she felt only soft curls. She reached around. The left braid hung down to her waist as it did every morning, but the right braid was gone.

That can't be, she thought.

But at the dresser, the mirror confirmed it. On one side, her hair was pulled back and braided properly; on the other it stuck out in unruly curls. And there, next to her brush and comb, lay a braided rope of hair, dark brown.

5

A Boy's Clothing

Vallie's throat went dry. Harold.

She closed her eyes and imagined him creeping into her room, hiding in the shadows. How long had he lurked, waiting, watching her sleep? Minutes, or hours? Surely Aunt Margaret wouldn't take his side this time. And she couldn't blame the cat for a chopped-off braid.

No, Vallie decided. *She'll blame me. Somehow this will be my fault.* A sour taste rose from her stomach, and she stared into the mirror. A changed face stared back. On the right side of her head, instead of a neat braid, her hair fluffed out in a dark halo.

She tugged at the curls, muttering, "Darn you, Harold. If you'd cut it any shorter, I'd look like a boy, not just a lopsided girl."

Vallie stepped closer to the silvered glass. Studying the image in the mirror, she took a deep breath. "I'd look like a boy . . . ," she repeated. Her thoughts drifted back to that train depot and the way people had fussed at her and made her feel weak and foolish.

"I'm not weak. I'm not scared or foolish either." She reached into her top drawer for her sewing scissors and felt the weight of cool steel in her hands. "All right, so be it. I'll be a boy, a raggedy boy who can take the train to Denver and find his father. So there!"

Vallie lifted the scissors, took a deep breath to steady her hand and snipped off the right braid. Again and again, she hacked at her hair. Then she plunged her hands into her washbowl and splashed water on her head, running her fingers through the mess and hoping the curls would hide any bare places. *Now what?*

No school and no breakfast either, not with Aunt Margaret or Uncle Franklin. And she absolutely refused to face Harold. She'd just have to get past Bridget.

She crawled back under her coverlet and tried to imagine what she'd need to travel west. Food, money, tickets. Those, she could manage. Clothing would be harder. She'd pack her own clothes in a box for when she found her father. But to travel as a boy, she needed shirts and trousers and didn't have any.

When the solution came, she could feel a smile spreading across her face. She'd raid Harold's cupboard, make off with his favorite shirts, and he wouldn't dare tell.

"Valentine, you awake yet?" Bridget knocked firmly on the door, opened it and peered in. "What, still in bed?"

"I don't feel too good," Vallie said.

Bridget rushed over, carrying Maria in her arms. "Well, you'll be wanting your doll then, to keep you company. Oh, goodness gracious, what's happened to your head?" She set down Maria and took Vallie by the shoulders, lifting her from the pillows.

"Oh, Vallie, girl. If you wanted a Titus haircut, you should have been asking your aunt first. She won't like it."

"It wasn't my idea, Bridget. Harold sneaked in while I was sleeping. Look, over on the dresser. He snipped off the first braid, I just finished the job."

Bridget picked up one chopped braid, then the second. "Oh, that boy. More wicked every day, he is. You'd think in a family this fine, he could share a bit of the attention, wouldn't you? But no, he's got to be the only star in the heavens. And won't his mother close her eyes again, I declare." She strode back to the bed and gripped Vallie's shoulder. "What will we tell her, girl?"

"I . . . I need time to think. Let's not tell her anything right away, please."

"She'll have to know," Bridget began. "But informing the missus is not a task I relish. So if you're wanting an hour or two to get ready for her scolding . . ."

Vallie hugged Maria. "Thanks. And I can't go to school today, Bridget. I just can't."

"Aye. And you won't have to. Oh, my Valentine, sure and didn't your da leave me here to watch over you, lass? I'll tell the missus you're feeling poorly, and I won't be tampering with the truth either. Now stay put and I'll bring you an invalid's breakfast."

Bridget bustled off. Vallie threw back the coverlet and jumped from the bed. Today's trains left the Allegheny depot at twelve-thirty and one-fifteen for Chicago and points west. One way or another she'd be aboard.

She opened her cupboard and looked at her dresses. Bridget had stitched up three new ones for spring, the yellow gingham she'd worn yesterday, a pale rose stripe, and a navy-and-white dress with a sailor's collar. She'd need a largish box, by the time she added underclothing and petticoats, slippers and stockings.

She'd also need underclothing for when she dressed as a boy, Vallie realized. But not Harold's, that would be too nasty. She thought hard and riffled through her cupboard, stopping when she reached her outgrown winter pantalets. She pulled them out and laid them across her bed. If she snipped off the legs and removed the ruffles and lace . . . Well, they'd just have to do. She got out her sewing scissors and began to cut.

Voices from the hall made her sit up and listen hard. Uncle Franklin sounded loud and cranky. "If it isn't one thing it's another, Margaret. Enough's enough."

"Now, Franklin. The poor child can't help it if she's ill."

"She's not our child, Margaret. A week or so is one thing. But sixteen months . . . That brother of yours should return home immediately and shoulder his responsibilities."

The familiar argument made Vallie want to hide under the pillows. She wished she weren't such a burden, especially to Aunt Margaret. Except where Harold was concerned, Aunt Margaret had always been kind. Too kind, if Bridget was right. It had made Harold jealous.

"Daniel will return when his heart has healed and his pockets are full."

"Humpf!" Uncle Franklin snorted. A door slammed.

A gentle knock came at her door. "Vallie, dear, may I come in?"

Vallie thought fast. "Indisposed, Aunt Margaret. I'm using the nightjar. Not feeling well. Might be catching." She made herself sit absolutely still. *Please, please don't come in.*

Aunt Margaret opened the door a tiny crack and spoke through it. "Now, dear, I'm sorry you're ill. I've promised the day to the literary society, but I'll send a note and cancel my plans." Out in the hall, Uncle Franklin moved about loudly again.

"Please, Aunt Margaret. Don't cancel."

"But if you're ill . . ."

"I just need some rest. Bridget will take good care of me. I'm sure I'll feel better by tomorrow." Vallie coughed.

"All right, but I'll come home early. Now you must rest. Drink lots of hot tea."

"Yes, ma'am. I will." *Please, please go downstairs.* After what seemed like days, Aunt Margaret walked away. As soon as she left for her literary society and Bridget was busy with her chores, Vallie could gather what she needed and sneak out.

Half an hour later, Bridget brought breakfast on a tray and sat while Vallie ate. "You look lovely, actually. But such short hair is unusual for a girl. How shall we explain it to the missus? She's so prim."

"I don't know. Please, don't fuss over me. I'm not really sick."

"Well, I'd be sick if somebody came creeping into my room by night, I would." Bridget shook her head.

"Maria will cheer me up," Vallie said. "You fixed her beautifully. You've . . . you've been so good to me, Bridget."

"Aye, and don't you need somebody, you poor wee

babe?" She mussed Vallie's curls. "Still, I have a day's work to do. You'll be all right?"

Vallie nodded. She reached out and hugged Bridget, tight as she could. She couldn't say so, but she hoped Bridget would understand later on, that this was goodbye. Just the thought made Vallie's throat sting.

When Vallie heard the creak of the pump in the backyard, she sped to the attic trunk room, then to Harold's bedroom. Minutes later she closed the lid of a wooden box she'd stuffed with her girl clothes, Maria, Papa's letters, photographs and clean writing paper. She hefted the box. Heavy, but not impossible.

She pulled on blue trousers and a white shirt and cuffed up the trouser legs. Slipping the shirt up, she tied four of her gold eagles into their money belt, knotted it around her middle and tucked the shirt back into the trousers. She checked the mirror, hoping the money belt didn't show, but the shirt was thick, sturdy cotton and hid her secrets well. She smiled at her reflection. "You make a tolerable-looking boy," she told herself. Getting dressed had been so easy and so quick. No wonder Harold was never late for church.

Vallie strode about the room, feeling light and free without all the petticoats. She tossed her head, which also felt light without the weight of long braids. She stowed a change of boy's clothing and a warm sweater in a faded carpetbag satchel. In a clean handkerchief, she wrapped one gold eagle and her small coins, stuffing them into a deep front trouser pocket with the folded-up train schedule. Nice, she thought, trousers came equipped with plenty of pockets for stowing things, which left a person's hands free.

She slipped into her oxfords, tied the laces and rechecked the mirror. *Time to go,* she thought.

Vallie listened at the door but couldn't hear Bridget moving around below. She peered out the window to the backyard in time to see the glint of water splashing from the dishpan. Kitchen chores were done, but since Vallie was never at home on school mornings, she didn't know what Bridget did next or where she'd be.

When in doubt, be cautious, Vallie decided. She shoved the box and the satchel under the bed and dove under the covers, carefully tucking in all signs of Harold's clothes. Knowing Bridget, she'd surely come back to check on Vallie. Soon footsteps creaked on the stairs.

Bridget popped her head in the door and smiled. "I'll just be tidying the rooms now. Shall I be changing your sheets? Would a fresh set calm your spirits?"

"No, thanks. I'd like to sleep. Last night was so upsetting. . . ."

"Last night was wickedness," Bridget said. "I'll be finding a way to show that boy the cost of his bad behavior." She closed the door and Vallie could hear her cross the hall to Aunt Margaret's room.

It was now or not at all. Vallie hopped from bed, gathered her belongings and carried them downstairs and out to the back alley. Setting her box under a bush, she hurried to the kitchen, where she loaded bread, cheese, apples and Bridget's famous ginger cookies into the satchel. At the last moment, she grabbed a packet of leftover ham slices and a sealed-up bottle of milk from the icebox. Bridget would notice the missing food, but with everybody gone for the day, who would she tell?

Vallie took one last look around the kitchen, ran her hand along the still-warm top of the stove, then turned from the room and hurried outside, blinking hard. "I love you, Bridget," she whispered to the kitchen door. "But I have to go. I'm sorry."

6

A Boy with a Box

Vallie lifted the wooden box to her shoulder, wishing she had enough spare coins to hire a hack to drive her to the depot. But hacks cost too much, so she'd have to walk.

She shifted the weight from her right to her left shoulder, gripped her satchel tightly and set off. The box was bulky and hard to balance. And Vallie didn't dare dawdle; the hall clock had been striking ten when she raided the kitchen. Yesterday the walk hadn't seemed terribly long, but yesterday she hadn't been weighed down.

When she reached the park and the train tracks, she ducked behind some bushes and set down her box. Catching her breath, she slipped her hand into her left pocket. She'd stuck her braids and the loose hair clippings in a spare handkerchief and jammed them into the pocket so that her aunt and uncle wouldn't guess she was traveling as a boy.

With a flick of her wrist the handkerchief opened, scattering braids and curls into the weeds. Perhaps some bird might weave bits of her hair into a nest; anyway, good riddance. She'd travel freer without it.

Forty-five hot, sweaty minutes later, she finally reached the depot, and as she stared at the fancy building her courage began to seep away. Yesterday had been bad enough and she'd just been playing hooky. Today was even worse—she was skipping school and impersonating a boy and running away from home.

The nasty grin of the ticket seller returned to her mind. She remembered all those men who had criticized her for coming to the depot alone. And those suspicious yard bulls. Whatever made her think she could fool such people? She'd never succeed in traveling as a boy. She hadn't the slightest idea how to act like one.

Of course you do, whispered a voice in her mind. *You've been stuck living in the same house with Harold for more than a year. You're even wearing his clothes. Act the way he does.*

"I can do that," she whispered back under her breath. Straightening her shoulders, she wrestled her heavy box inside the double doors and strode to the ticket booth. From across the room she could see the same ticket seller as yesterday. She cleared her throat to lower her voice, threw back her shoulders even more, as if carrying the box didn't hurt in the least, and strolled boldly up to the man.

"Ticket to Chicago, one way." If people came looking for her, they'd be after a girl going to Denver, not a boy heading for Chicago, so she'd buy tickets as she needed them. She watched as the man counted her money.

"Okay, bub, here's your ticket," he said. "Number Seventeen leaves at twelve-thirty. Track one. You got a box there, best tie some twine around it. And mark it with your name and destination. Can't be too careful." He tossed Vallie a hank of twine and a thick pencil.

"Thanks." She swaggered off toward a bench to take care of her box. Inside, a laugh bubbled up. He'd called her bub and talked to her like a regular traveling person, not like some baby who didn't know how to behave. He was the same man she'd seen yesterday, but from his conversation, you'd never know it. Being a boy had advantages.

Lifting her box and turning toward the ladies' waiting room, Vallie nearly spoiled the whole masquerade. *I can't go in there now,* she realized with a start. Quickly she found a bench in the main waiting room, closer to the tracks, and settled in to watch the people.

A man took the bench across from her and opened

a paper sack. He pulled out the end of a sausage and a knife from his pocket and began to carve slices and pop them into his mouth. He chewed loudly, with his mouth open. A strong, sour scent of sausage drifted across the benches.

Nothing at Papa's or Aunt Margaret's house had prepared Vallie for this ill-mannered behavior. She looked away, her appetite gone, but she couldn't change benches again; that would look suspicious.

The man ate the whole sausage, slowly. When he'd finished, he wiped his greasy hands on his trousers. Then he began to clean his fingernails with the knife. She wondered if he'd eat so rudely if she were wearing her girl clothes. But then if she were wearing girl clothes, shc could sit in the ladies' waiting room, far away from the nasty fellow. Well, it was only a short wait. If she got lucky, he'd be riding a different train or at least a different car.

As she sat there, a train pulled into the depot with a rush of smoke and a screeching of brakes. People milled around. A trainman called out in a loud voice, "Eastbound train arriving from Chicago. Track two. All aboard for Johnstown, Altoona, Harrisburg and Philadelphia."

Two of those yard bulls watched passengers climb down from the cars with their belongings. Vallie tried to shrink down and become invisible. But the ticket seller had called her bub. If she hid she'd look guilty and they'd surely sniff out her secret. She sat straighter.

The sausage man pulled a plug of tobacco from his jacket pocket and sliced off a large chunk. With a grin, he offered it to her.

She shook her head, trying not to grimace. "No, thanks."

He shrugged, stuck the whole thing in his mouth and began to chew. Vallie knew what was coming. She edged backward until her spine pressed against the back of the bench. She pulled her feet underneath as far as she could and looked away.

Soon she heard it. *Splat!* Tobacco juice landed right next to her shoe. She took one deep breath, then a second, fighting the urge to find a rag and scrub her shoe. The ladies' waiting room might as well be a million miles away.

Vallie patted her wooden box and traced the words on top: V. E. HARPER, ASPEN, COLORADO. She sat there trying to look ordinary while another train arrived and left in a cloud of soot and smoke and noise. The depot clock above the ticket booth read noon. The man sat on his bench as if he'd been planted. At last he stood and ambled toward the men's necessary.

Vallie hadn't eaten or drunk anything since leaving Aunt Margaret's at about ten. Between her nerves and the sausage man's rude behavior, she wasn't hungry, but she really needed a trip to the necessary. Just not the men's. She'd have to wait; she crossed her fingers and hoped the train would have small comfort rooms, meant for one person at a time.

"Number Seventeen. Arriving, track number one." A loud voice boomed out, making Vallie sit up quickly. "Continuing west in ten minutes. Track number one. All aboard for Fort Wayne, Chicago and points west."

Do I really dare? she wondered.

7

Aboard

Vallie squirmed on the bench and took a deep breath. *If I go, Aunt Margaret will be upset. Bridget will never forgive me. And Papa might be glad to see me, or he might be angry because I've come before he's ready.* She ran her fingers along her bare neck and chopped hair. *But if I stay I'll miss Papa more and more, and Harold will get bolder and bolder.*

She closed her eyes, remembering her cousin's nasty grin. Staying was worse, she decided.

"Give 'em room now, give 'em room." A trainman waved the crowd back from the tracks as arriving passengers climbed down the metal steps.

As Vallie stood and hoisted her box to her shoulder it shifted, almost slipping out of her grasp. She yanked on it, banging her shoulder. Pain shot down her arm, but she held on. If the box fell and popped open, people would see girl's clothing. No matter how heavy, she had to get it onto the train.

At last the steps cleared. "Aboard," the trainman called.

From all directions people shoved toward the doors. Vallie shoved along with them. Somebody stepped on her foot. From behind, a valise banged her leg. When she reached the stairs, she hurried up.

"Pullman to the front, coach to the rear. Pullman to the front, coach to the rear," the trainman droned.

Vallie trudged through the first coach car and searched for an empty seat. Most of the benches had people or belongings spread over them. The second car looked much the same. In the third car, she spotted an empty bench and sped toward it. From behind, someone shoved her and crowded past, taking the bench. It was the sausage man from the station. Fine, she'd happily take another car to avoid him.

She hurried back farther and found herself a seat in the fourth coach car. She set her box down on the bench and plopped down beside it. A woman with a small child marched up. "Seat taken?"

"Um . . ."

"V. E. Harper. What's the V. E. stand for?"

Vallie swallowed hard. What should she say? Valentine wasn't a common name, but she'd heard it used for boys as well as girls. She didn't dare admit to the Elizabeth, though. "Valentine Edward," she mumbled.

"Born in February, I suppose. What some people think of." The woman tapped the box. "Baggage goes up on the shelf, boy. Train's crowded."

"Yes, ma'am." Vallie had to climb onto the bench to reach. She had to shove the box hard to get it onto the shelf.

"Here," the woman said, passing up two valises and a large parcel before Vallie could climb down. One of the valises felt as if it had been packed full of bricks, and it wobbled as Vallie tried to hoist it onto the shelf.

"Watch that bag," the woman said. "Don't be clumsy, now."

"Yes, ma'am," Vallie repeated, scowling to herself at the woman's rudeness. She bit her tongue to keep from complaining, though. Maybe boys were just supposed to help strangers and not ask questions. Sliding into the seat, she pulled her satchel onto her lap and peered out the window. Once they left the depot, she'd watch the country slide past.

The woman fussed with the child's clothing and settled into the seat. The child turned out to be a little girl with straight black hair and black eyes. She stuck her thumb in her mouth and peered at Vallie.

"Tickets! Tickets! Take your seats now, take your seats." A conductor made his way along the aisle as people crowded in and crammed their belongings onto the overhead shelves.

Vallie fumbled in her pocket for her ticket. The conductor punched a hole in it and poked it into a little slot in the back of the next seat.

"Where's the necessary, please, sir?"

"Last car. But it stays locked until we leave town. When you see green fields out your window, you can use the facilities, not before. Should have used the depot."

She crossed her legs tightly. "Yes, sir. Green fields. Thanks." Vallie sighed and tried to think dry thoughts. Was this the way an adventure was supposed to start, she wondered, with a full bladder and an empty stomach?

After several more minutes of jostling people and thumping baggage, the whistle blew and a trainman marched along, rechecking tickets and slamming the doors between the cars. The whistle blew again and the train jolted forward in a great clacking of wheels.

Out the window, the depot fence drifted backward as the train picked up speed. Soon Vallie could see Pittsburgh on one side and Allegheny City on the other. Buildings sped by so fast they did strange things to her stomach. She was really doing it, she was leaving home. Everyone and everything she knew slid away in a blur, leaving an empty ache inside. *Oh, Bridget, I'll write soon. I promise.* Vallie squeezed her eyes shut and whispered to herself, "I'm coming, Papa, coming West to see you. Please be glad."

By the time she could see those green fields, Vallie was sure she'd burst. On unsteady legs, she hurried to the rear of the train. She had to swing open heavy doors and step into the place between the cars where the wind blew, and she could see below the coupling joint to where the earth slipped past. It made her stomach swim.

When she finally reached the end of the train, three people were standing in line. That meant another five minutes to wait, but at least they had a necessary. And it must be small because folks were entering and leaving one at a time. She wouldn't get found out—if she could make it in time.

At last it was her turn. The necessary looked like a fancy privy on wheels. Across from the one-seater, a small wood barrel hung from the wall, with a spigot and basin for washing up and a sign that said: NOTIFY TRAINMAN IF WATER RUNS LOW—PLEASE EMPTY BASIN AND TIDY UP AFTER USING.

Vallie obeyed the sign, glad to rinse her hands and face. On her return through the cars, she walked slowly, letting her legs roll with the train's noisy motion. *It's easy to swagger here,* she thought. *I'm like a sailor with his sea legs.* Tossing her head back, she wondered if there were such things as train legs, and if she'd get them after a week on the rails. That would be something to write Bridget about.

When she reached her bench, the woman had moved over and now sat next to the window.

"Pardon me, please," Vallie said. "That's my seat."

"Prissy, ain't ya?"

Vallie's breath caught—she'd talked like a girl and nearly given everything away. She glared at the woman and tried for a deeper voice. "You grabbed my seat and I want it back."

"But surely you would allow a lady such as myself to watch out the window, wouldn't you?"

"But lady . . ."

The little girl looked from her mother to Vallie and back again, her thumb still in her mouth.

"I'd like to look out the window," the woman said. "A young boy such as yourself could find another seat, while my baby and I . . ."

Of all the nerve. Harold wasn't the only bully in this world.

The woman glowered and huffed as if she were some fancy society lady. "You obviously are a brash boy. You'll never make a gentleman unless you mend your rude ways."

Vallie sank into the aisle seat. Suddenly it was all she could do not to burst out laughing. *I'll never make a gentleman no matter what,* she thought. She sat and turned her face away, afraid the woman might read her mind or continue scolding. *But* I *have been well brought up,* Vallie decided. *No lady* I *ever met would snitch a person's seat. Especially a person who had so kindly lifted all that baggage up to the rack.*

One good thing, the woman had opened the train's window, so cooler air blew in. It smelled of spring fields and damp grass and farms. Another smell mixed in, coal smoke, bringing dust and grit.

I hope she gets soot all over her dress, sitting by that darn window, Vallie thought. She shifted on the bench and reached for her satchel. Suddenly her stomach was rumbling, shouting for food. She pulled out two slices of ham, a heel of bread and her bottle of milk. She'd finished the first slice of ham when she felt tiny fingers tug on her shirtsleeve.

Vallie peeked over at the woman, but her head nodded with the train's swaying and her eyes were closed. So much for looking out the window. Vallie winked at the little girl and broke off a small bite of bread and another of ham. The tiny fingers snatched them up and stuffed them into the mouth. The child tried to wink back, but instead of one eye, she opened and shut both several times, reminding Vallie of a small, wise bird.

Vallie fed the little girl a few more bites, and between them, they finished the food. When Vallie reached into her satchel for one of Bridget's ginger cookies, the little eyes followed right along. Vallie broke off a chunk of cookie and passed it to the child, ate the rest and downed half the bottle of milk. Vallie brushed crumbs from the round, warm cheeks, and the little girl smiled. Then she curled up and nestled into

Vallie's side, one small hand patting Vallie's knee in time to the clacking music of the train's wheels.

The girl was sweet, reminding Vallie of the little boy in the backyard of her old house. A soreness pressed in on Vallie's chest. These babies were so lucky, she thought, they had their mothers around to love them and look after them.

Bridget does that for me, Vallie realized. *And even Aunt Margaret's not so bad. But I've left them behind. I've got nobody but myself for a while, and whatever strangers, rude or kind, I meet on my journey.*

Vallie took a deep breath. Feeling sorry for herself wouldn't get her to Colorado any sooner. Besides, in a few days she'd find her father, and he'd hug her so hard, it would make everything all right again.

Between now and then, she could make a list in her mind of funny things and odd people to cheer herself up. Then, when she found Papa, she'd have tales to tell. So far she had three names for a list in just one afternoon: Sausage Man, Grumpy Woman, Sweet Hungry Girl. She leaned back and watched out the window as the mountains softened into hills and the sun began its slow slide into the western sky.

The train jerked to a stop in Rochester and again in New Brighton, letting off and taking on passengers. They stopped next in Alliance, Ohio, for coal and water. *Ohio.* Vallie repeated the state's name softly, and as she did, a stiffness she hadn't even noticed seemed to slip away from her shoulders.

By now they probably knew she was missing and were beginning to search, but she'd done it. She'd left Pennsylvania and her troubles behind.

From now on, I'll have to be extra careful, she thought, but still, her heart lifted. *Here I come, Papa. Here I come.*

8

In Disguise

As the sky changed from blue to rose, hills gave way to rolling farms. Pinpricks of lamplight shone from farmhouse windows. The train rattled along the tracks, stopping often as they passed through Ohio. Somewhere after the town of Lima, Vallie leaned into her bench and let the rocking of the train lull her to sleep.

She woke to the sound of raised voices and people bustling. The sun was up, which meant they must be nearing Chicago. Vallie jumped to her feet and scurried to the rear of the train for the necessary before they locked it up. Pretending to be a boy could be such a bother.

When she returned to her seat, the woman had pulled her valises down. The little girl patted Vallie's hand. The woman snatched the child's fingers back and scolded. "Leave that rough boy alone. He could be dirty."

But I just washed, Vallie thought. She didn't argue, though; soon she'd leave Grumpy Woman behind. *Maybe I'll leave the rough boy behind too,* she decided, *if I can find a place to change clothes.*

She peered up at her box. Not a good idea. Even as the train slowed, she could see the dark uniforms and shiny brass buttons of those railroad police. Uncle Franklin had been busy.

She grabbed for her box and her satchel, then let her eyes rest on Grumpy Woman. *I don't like her, but she can help me,* Vallie figured. When the car finally came to a stop, she shadowed the woman and child, trying to look as if she belonged to their family. On the platform she took long, swaggering steps like a boy. With the heavy box on her shoulder, it wasn't easy. And those yard bulls were everywhere. At least Grumpy Woman didn't walk very fast.

In an archway, Vallie spotted a porter with an empty cart. "Excuse me," she said gruffly. "Train to Denver?"

The man pulled a gold watch from his pocket and flipped it open. "Track six. Train's about to leave. You might make it if you hurry. That way." He pointed.

"I don't have a ticket," she said.

"Buy one on the train." The porter turned to assist a tall woman with several fancy trunks.

Vallie stumbled in the direction he'd pointed, up a

set of stairs toward another endless track. Here too, yard bulls patrolled, thick as bees in Aunt Margaret's flower garden. *I have to make that train,* Vallie realized. Waiting around in the depot would be impossible. With the box wobbling on her shoulder, she shoved past the crowds and flung herself into the doorway of a railroad car. A trainman with a red face was yanking on the vestibule door.

"Denver?"

"Yep. Get aboard, we're pulling out soon as I shut this door."

Vallie staggered into the car, giddy. Out the window, she could see two yard bulls watching the train and puffing on fat black cigars. She'd done it; she'd escaped!

Scanning the car, she saw a free seat next to an old man with a full white beard. Safe enough; to Vallie's eye, he looked like somebody's grandfather. She hauled herself and her belongings along the aisle.

As she lifted her box to the overhead rack, she noticed the words she'd written on the top—V. E. HARPER, ASPEN, COLORADO. Vallie winced—she might as well be wearing a sign around her neck. First chance she got, she'd scribble over her name. For now, all she could do was turn the box on its side so that the writing faced backward and hope nobody snooped. So careless!

Her right hand was smudged with dirt from the bottom of the box, and she started to wipe it on her trousers, then stopped. Instead, she rubbed it on her cheek. If Aunt Margaret could see her, she'd pitch a fit, but the dirt felt good, like a mask. It improved her disguise.

When the conductor came around, Vallie bought a ticket from Chicago to Omaha and on to Denver. As the man punched her ticket and stuck it into its slot, Vallie figured her money again. Train tickets were expensive—she'd just spent another twenty-four dollars and fifty cents. Four of her gold eagles had flown since yesterday morning, but she had seventeen sixty-five to get her from Denver to Aspen, so money wasn't her biggest worry. The yard bulls were. She had to find out if any of those sharp-eyed policemen had boarded this train.

After taking three deep breaths to calm down, she looked around at her fellow passengers. The old man next to her was staring out the window. He didn't appear the least bit scary. "Excuse me, sir," she began.

"Hello there, boy-o," said the whiskered man. "You're looking better. Thought you might lose your dinner there for a while."

Seeing those yard bulls, she must have let her face go all girlish and scared. Another mistake.

"I'm fine," Vallie lied, making sure her voice sounded deep and rough. "Just wondered. Seen a commotion in Chicago. Police all around the depot. Did something happen?"

"Not that I know of. Police always patrol. All those

crowds, don't you know. Travelers who don't watch their pockets. Ripe pickings."

"How about the trains? Do police ride to protect travelers?" She tried to ask her questions in a nosy way, without sounding worried or guilty.

The man scratched his beard. His eyebrows twitched. "Them yard bulls stay in the depots," he began. He lowered his voice. "It's the Pinkertons who ride the trains."

"Pinkertons?"

"Private detectives. Couple of them ride each and every train."

"Really? That makes a person feel . . . real safe." Vallie's heart beat double time again. "They wear dark blue uniforms too? Like the police?" She scanned the car anxiously.

"Huh! You're a green one, you are," Mr. White Whiskers replied. He twitched his eyebrows again. "Pinkertons travel in disguise," he whispered. "They're watching out for shenanigans, so they don't want to call attention to themselves."

He pointed across the aisle toward a man wearing a rough jacket and dirty boots. "See that young fella over there. Looks like a farmer, don't he? But he might just be a Pinkerton. Or that slicked-up gent near the back, with his salesman's samples. He could be watching this very car."

"I . . . I see." Vallie had a hard time swallowing. "What are they watching for, these Pinkertons?"

"Sometimes they're on special assignment, but mostly they watch the trainmen. Now and again, a conductor might forget to write down a fare, don't you know. Might slip your money into his own pocket instead of the cash box. Pinkerton detective, he'll catch that, quick as a cat."

Special assignment. That could be me. Vallie's throat went dry. She reached for her bottle of water.

Mr. White Whiskers pulled a brown bottle from his pocket, tugged out the cork and offered it to her. "Like a nip? Asking all those questions parches a fella's throat, don't it?"

What would a boy do? "A . . . a nip? No, thanks." And no more questions either. She'd asked too many already.

"Still a green boy-o, huh?"

"Yes, sir. I . . . I promised my . . . my grandma. She's a temperance lady. She'd . . ." Oh, the lies . . .

"She'd tan your hide, huh? Well, you're young yet. Whiskey'll keep. Nothing like it for a powerful thirst." The man took a long drink, then stuck the cork back into the bottle. He wiped his mouth and combed his fingers through his beard as if to tidy it. "Tell you what, boy-o. You passed my test. You're a good sort. Not a scalawag."

"Yes, sir," Vallie mumbled. She sipped water from her bottle and swallowed.

"Good thing too." The man's eyes filled with mischief. "Who knows? Under this here beard, I myself might be one of them Pinkerton men."

Vallie tried to smile. She glanced up at her box in the rack above her head. From now until she found her father, no more mistakes. Careful would be her middle name.

9

Guttersnipes

"Omaha, Omaha next."

Vallie must have fallen asleep because she jumped at the announcement. Her neck felt stiff. All around her, people were bustling and readying themselves for the depot.

In her satchel Vallie had only a little cheese left, and one apple, so she'd need to buy food here in Omaha. As she climbed down to the crowded platform with her satchel in hand, she found herself face-to-face with another of those yard bulls, a pale, frowning fellow with a dark mustache. Scurrying behind two large men, she ducked toward a stairway. From above, she heard voices calling, "Coffee! Hot buns!" and raced up some stairs and around a corner, then stopped short.

A skinny boy with messy blond hair held a small,

dirty boy with one arm, choking him hard. The little boy struggled and coughed—beneath the smudges his face was bright red.

Another grimy boy stood nearby, digging into his trouser pocket.

"What's going on?" Vallie demanded.

The three of them looked at her. The mean one was half a head shorter than she was and he didn't look any too strong.

Stepping closer, she yanked hard on the boy's bony arm. "Let go of him."

He pulled away from her, scowling. "Mind your own business."

"I got your nickel," said the boy who'd been searching his pockets. "Now let my brother loose."

Fire rose in Vallie's heart, her fingers balled up. This was Harold all over again—that made it her business. And she didn't have to cower behind her skirts. She was bigger than this bully! She hauled back and punched the boy right in the face. He let go of the smaller boy, took a long look at Vallie and swore, then ran toward the stairway, holding his nose.

She looked at her hand as if it belonged to somebody else. She'd really socked the boy.

"Here you go, buster." The bigger of the brothers held out the nickel.

"I'm not after your money."

"What you want then?" the little one asked.

"Nothing." Vallie's breath was coming out in short, shaky bursts. *I socked him, I really did it.* "I just . . . I knew a bully back home. He picked on me. I hated it." She ran her fingers through her short hair.

"You sure?" The grubby hand still stretched out, a single coin in the palm.

"Keep your money. I've got some."

"What you doing here then?" the little one asked.

"Hush, Joseph. Don't bother him."

"Traveling." Vallie stuck out her hand. "Pleased to meet you, Joseph."

Joseph grinned and shook her hand. "He's my brother, Patrick is."

She shook Patrick's hand. It felt thin; even the bones seemed light, birds' bones instead of boys'. "Are you traveling?"

"Nope. We live here," Joseph said.

"Shh," Patrick warned.

"Here in Omaha?" Vallie smiled at the little boy, Joseph. He looked about seven. Patrick might be eight or nine.

Joseph shook his head. "We live in the depot. Trainmen call us guttersnipes."

"But that's impossible. Nobody lives in train depots."

"We do," he bragged. "And we live real fine too."

"Joseph," Patrick said. "Quit blabbing." He frowned at Vallie.

"I won't tell," she said. "I've got secrets myself." From the tracks below, a train whistled, and the motion made the floor vibrate beneath her feet. "What's that? Is a new train coming in?"

"Nope. That's the Denver train, heading west," Patrick said.

"No! It can't be!" Vallie whirled and flew down the steps. The platform had emptied of people, and as she reached the tracks, she could see the last cars of a train speed past. "No!" she shouted again.

Joseph ran toward her with Patrick two steps behind. "What train was you on?"

Vallie closed her eyes tight. "That one. Now I've missed it."

"You can stay with us," Joseph offered.

"But I . . . My . . ." Vallie's words stuck in her throat. She kicked at a pillar that stood near the track. "Darn it all!"

Patrick stepped closer and frowned. "Did you get lost from your people? Did your family leave you behind?"

"No. I . . . I was traveling alone. To the Rocky Mountains to find my pa. But my box . . ." She looked down at the carpetbag satchel she clutched in her left hand. "My box was on that train."

"Did your box have important things in it?" Joseph asked.

It had everything, Vallie realized. Her girl clothes, Papa's letters, the photographs—every real and important item she owned was rolling toward Denver while she stood here in Omaha. She kicked the pillar again, harder, and it made her toe sting.

"You got your ticket?" Patrick asked.

"My ticket! No!" Vallie stuck her hand into her pocket, but she knew it was hopeless. Her ticket was still sitting in a little slot on the back of the next seat, on its way to Denver without her. Her heart was thumping as fast as train wheels. Before, she'd made little mistakes. This was enormous. "I left my ticket on the train! Now what am I going to do?"

"Buy another ticket?" the littler boy suggested.

"I . . . I can't. I don't have enough money." Vallie poked her hand into her pocket again, fingering the small coins. If she spent her last golden eagle on another ticket to Denver, she'd never make it from Denver to Aspen.

"You can stay with us," Joseph said again.

Vallie looked around at the grimy walls and filthy platform. Yard bulls patrolled this depot—they'd catch her for sure. Even here, down by the tracks, she didn't feel safe. She edged closer to the shadowy wall, wondering what would become of her. She'd been absolutely careless and now she'd pay for it.

"I can't stay here. I need to go west. I need money, lots of it."

"Do what we do, then," the older boy said.

"Which is?"

"Haul valises. Come on." He pointed toward the stairs.

"I . . . I couldn't take your work."

"Quit lollygagging," Patrick said. "Come on."

Her heart still pounding, Vallie followed the boys upstairs and outside to where hacks were pulling up and letting out passengers. She slipped the handles of her satchel across her shoulder, freeing both hands. Then she glanced back to see if anybody was watching her. Nobody was. Not yet.

"Carry your grip, sir?" Joseph asked. "Me and my"—he winked at Vallie—"me and my brothers, we're plenty strong."

The man nodded, and Vallie found herself helping Patrick drag a large trunk while Joseph hefted a small leather satchel. They followed the man to the ticket booth, then into the waiting room. He tossed Vallie a coin. "I'm catching the eleven o'clock train on track three. Come back in a couple of hours and you can earn another dime."

Vallie rolled the coin in her hand. One thin dime and it wasn't even all hers. She'd have to haul hundreds of trunks to earn enough for a ticket.

"Yessir," Patrick told the man. "You can count on us." He turned and headed back toward the entrance. Vallie passed him the dime.

He shook his head. "Naw, you keep it for now. We'll divide later."

As she worked alongside the boys, Vallie glanced around, checking the whereabouts of the railroad police, but they weren't paying her any attention. She took a deep breath and tried to stop worrying but her troubles weighed heavy on her shoulders. On top of everything else, she was hungry. "When can we eat? I'm starving."

"Wait for the eleven o'clock. Then it gets real quiet."

After the train had come and gone and she'd used the privy meant for the yard crews, Vallie felt light and empty. "Can we please get some food?"

Patrick nodded. "Yep. But not at the depot. Costs too much. Come on." He led her across the tracks to a small market, where Joseph stepped up to the counter. "You got any of yesterday's bread? End hunks of cheese?"

The man behind the counter nodded and brought out some bread and cheese. He set down three bruised apples and a couple of dry carrots.

"How much?" Patrick asked.

"Thirty cents. You got an extra boy today." He looked Vallie over, and she tried not to flinch.

"Twenty cents," Patrick said. "Them apples are small."

"Two bits?" the man asked.

Patrick nodded toward Vallie, and she reached into her pocket. Their meal would come from the money they'd earned, which meant even less for a new ticket.

She could be stuck in Omaha forever. Outside again, they sat under a tree and shared the food. Vallie added the leavings from her satchel and tried to put her worries out of her mind for a while; otherwise she'd just puddle up and cry.

"Do you really live at the depot? What about your family?"

"We only got a ma," Patrick said slowly. "She drinks whiskey."

"But surely you go home to sleep."

"No. We sleep in the trunk room. It's warm there. Trunk man's nice."

"Nobody yells at the depot," Joseph added. "Or beats you with a switch, or throws empty bottles."

Joseph's words made Vallie's blood chill. Their home must be dreadful if a train depot was a better place to live. "But that bully . . ."

"He thinks he's some punkins," Patrick said. "But he ain't."

"Usually we run off before he can catch us. I was slow today," Joseph explained. "Food's gone. You want to go picking? Next train ain't till four."

"Picking what?" *Not pockets,* she hoped. *Please, not pockets.*

"This and that," Joseph answered. "You need money, don't you?"

"I guess." Vallie hefted her satchel and stood reluctantly. She couldn't afford to break any laws, but she did need money.

Patrick led the way through a maze of dusty alleyways. "Here's something," he said, stopping to lift a tin bucket. "We'll get a penny for this."

So this is picking, Vallie thought with relief. *Aunt Margaret would bust right out of her corset if she could see me now.* But it was surely safer to be outside earning pennies instead of sitting in the depot making the yard bulls suspicious. Vallie needed those pennies.

"Oh, look," Joseph said. "Somebody put out old sheets. The rag man will buy them." He turned to Vallie. "Can you help carry?"

"Sure." Vallie helped the boys scour the area.

They hauled their stash to the junk man and the rag man, then returned to the depot to carry luggage for the four o'clock eastbound train and the seven o'clock southbound. The day's work earned them about a dollar and a half, fifty cents for Vallie.

She worked the numbers in her head. At this rate she'd have to spend weeks here, she realized. There had to be another way.

10

Baggage

For supper, the boys begged leftover soup from a café. Vallie's feet dragged by the time they returned to the depot.

"You sure I can sleep here?" she asked. She didn't want to sit up all night in the waiting room, but getting the boys in trouble would be worse.

"The night man likes us. We'll tell him your ma drinks whiskey too." Joseph patted her arm.

Vallie shook her head, trying not to add up all the fibs she'd told. Still, she followed and let Joseph and Patrick tell whatever whoppers they wanted to.

In the trunk room, they climbed to a top shelf and unrolled thin, torn blankets. She took the sweater from her satchel and put it on, for the night was chilly. In one corner, she noticed a pile of shabby clothes. "Yours?"

"Spares," Patrick said. "I scrub one set so we don't

stink too bad. I sneak into the house early in the morning, before Ma's awake to catch me. Summers, we dunk in the river."

"Patrick's a smart brother," Vallie said to Joseph. "You're lucky."

And they *were* lucky in a strange sort of way, she thought as she buttoned her sweater. Having a mother who drank whiskey and yelled and threw bottles sounded terrible, but at least Joseph and Patrick had food to eat and a place to stay. And they had each other. *Which is more than I have,* she realized as she settled in to share their tattered blankets. *I have to get myself to Colorado, to find Papa, and soon.*

Using her satchel as a pillow, Vallie flopped this way and that on the shelf, trying to get comfortable. "I was wondering," she began. "Is there any other way for me to reach Denver? It will take forever to earn a new ticket. Maybe I could help out on the train or something."

"Let me think on it," Patrick said. "Maybe something will come to me."

Nothing came to Vallie as she squirmed on the hard shelf in the trunk room. But she didn't dare stay here long. Uncle Franklin had to be looking for her, and he'd have people scouring every depot from Pittsburgh to Denver. As the night wore on, she kept seeing her uncle's face, and Harold's, along with that neatly punched ticket sitting in its little shiny slot. The faces grinned at her as if to say, *You've been so foolish, you deserve to get caught.*

As the gray light of morning began to show in the trunk room's high windows, Vallie heard rustling from the boys on the shelves beside her.

"You'd best get up if you don't want to miss another train," Patrick called.

"But I still don't have a ticket," Vallie said. "And I bet nobody tossed a pile of money in here while we were sleeping."

"Look, Vallie, I got an idea. Joseph, you go find something to eat, fast."

Vallie sat up. "What's your idea?"

"It came to me in the night," Patrick explained. "I was looking at the shadows of this here trunk." He tapped the side of a big trunk next to him. "I bet you could sneak into the baggage car. It's at the very back of the train, and nobody but the porters and the trunk man go there."

"Sneak on?"

"You wouldn't be the first. We see plenty of shadows, jumping off as the trains slow down. You ain't big, you could hide there."

"But isn't it dishonest? Cheating the railroad?"

Patrick shrugged. "You bought a ticket, didn't you? You paid. They owe you a ride."

His words made sense. She'd never make enough money for a ticket by hauling luggage and picking trash. "I . . . I guess I'll try. Just hope I don't get caught."

"We'll help you," Patrick promised.

Joseph returned, wearing a big smile. He set a half loaf of bread, an end of sausage and three eggs down next to her while Patrick explained his idea again.

Joseph nodded and pointed at the eggs. "Hard-boiled. You can eat them in the baggage car."

"Thanks." Vallie reached out to hug Joseph but caught herself and punched him lightly on the shoulder instead, the way a real boy would. "Is there a pump? There won't be water in the baggage car, so I should fill up now."

"I'll show you," Joseph offered. He led Vallie outside, where she used the privy, splashed cold water on her face and filled her bottle with water.

Indoors again, Patrick met her at the doorway to the trunk room. His hands were behind his back.

"Come on, Pat, show him," Joseph urged.

Patrick smiled and pulled something from behind his back. He held it up to Vallie, a thick gray woolen jacket. "It's for you."

"We hear people talk. Them Rocky Mountains are real cold," Joseph explained. "Even in summer. You just got that thin sweater."

Patrick shoved the jacket into her hands. "Go on.

It's for you. Too big for us. We found it a couple of days ago, right here in the station."

"But you could sell it. Get money for food."

"We got enough," Patrick said. "We find lots of things to sell."

"Still—"

Patrick interrupted. "I've been thinking. When you get to Denver. That box you left on yesterday's train. It might be there. In the trunk room. You could ask."

"Thanks. That's a good idea," Vallie mumbled. And it was, except that if her box had been found, one of those Pinkertons would be guarding it by now. She couldn't ask about her belongings without getting caught.

"Try it on," Joseph said. "Try on the coat."

She slipped her arms into the sleeves. It was roomy, but if she turned up the cuffs, it fit fine. "It's beautiful." Her eyes filled and she brushed the dampness away, trying not to let her feelings show.

"What you doing? Are you crying?" Joseph asked.

Patrick stepped closer and stuck his face right in hers. "What's the matter with you? Crying like some pudding-faced girl?"

Suddenly it was all too much—the running and hiding, those awful yard bulls, the strangers on the trains, and now, two little boys who were being so kind. Vallie's eyes filled again. "I can't help it. I . . . I am a girl." She covered her face with her hands.

Patrick scowled and stared at her. Finally he spoke. "You . . . can't be. You fought off Dirty Eddie. A sissy girl couldn't do that."

Vallie chewed on her thumbnail. "I'm not a sissy, but I am a girl."

Joseph had taken a step backward. He glared. "How come? How come you're a girl if you're dressed like a boy?"

"I'm running away. Girls can't ride the trains alone. Boys can."

"But we don't like girls," Joseph said. "So we can't like you."

She sighed. "I'm sorry."

"You lied to us. You said you were going to the Rocky Mountains to find your pa," Patrick said.

"I am." Oh, why had she opened her big mouth?

"Who you running from, then? Your ma?"

Vallie shook her head. "Don't have one. It's my aunt. She—"

"Did she beat you?" Joseph asked.

"No. I just need to find my father. I'm sorry I made you think I was a boy. I've been telling a lot of whoppers. Can we still be friends? Please?"

Joseph studied her face for a long time as if he was making up his mind. Then he nodded. "You're like a bank robber. On the lam. We'll be your gang, sneak you on the baggage car, help you run from the sheriff."

"I guess," Vallie agreed. "Will you still help? And

keep my secret? If anybody finds out . . . They'll haul me back East."

"We ain't blabbers," Patrick said. "Come on. Train's due soon."

"Of course." Vallie understood. Patrick wanted to get rid of her, now that he knew she was a girl. She didn't much blame him, just hoped he could keep a secret better than she had. Still, telling the truth had felt good, like a weight coming off her shoulders. Besides, the boys had helped her so much, Vallie figured they deserved the real story. Grabbing her satchel, she followed them down the stairs and onto the farthest end of the platform.

Beside the tracks, Patrick seemed to want to keep his distance. Joseph wasn't bothered so much. "I been working this depot a long time, but I never sneaked a person on a train before, never even sent somebody off on a trip. Specially not a bank robber. Have a good ride, Vallie."

She mussed his hair, then shook Patrick's hand. "Thanks. I'll try. There is one thing, though. Would you ever . . . well, if things got bad here, would you want to come West? Once I find my papa, we could . . ."

Patrick shook his head. "We're fine. We gotta keep an eye on our ma."

"Right. That makes sense." Except that it didn't make sense. Their ma should be keeping an eye on them, not the other way around.

"Look smart now, train's about here. You hop on between the last passenger car and the baggage car, yank open the door and hide in the car before the trainman gets there."

"All right. How about getting off? How will I know when we get to Denver?"

"It's the last stop. A big town. You'll know."

With a jumble of smoke and noise, the train pulled into the depot, doors opened and people clambered out. The trainman shouted above the din, "Aboard. All aboard for Denver. Den-ver."

"Go on now, while it's crowded," Patrick said, shoving her toward the tracks. "And good luck."

"Thanks." Clutching her satchel to her chest, Vallie darted to the end of the train and jumped between the cars as Patrick had suggested. Nobody seemed to notice. She yanked on the door latch, pulling it down until she heard a click, then slid the door open and ducked inside. Hiding behind a large wooden crate, she tried to catch her breath.

The door opened again, and loud thumps told Vallie that something big was getting loaded or unloaded. She shrank down, cowering to make herself as small as possible, trying not to count up her mistakes.

It was so odd. She'd traveled all the way from Pennsylvania to Nebraska, ducking yard bulls and Pinkerton detectives, only to blab her secrets to two little boys. But they were smart, she realized. They knew how to find food and bargain and take care of themselves. So they'd take care of her secret too. At least she hoped so.

Little stray boys, guttersnipes, they'd called themselves. She'd been a guttersnipe too, she realized. And a ragpicker—*How about that, Aunt Margaret?* And when she'd pounded on the bully, she'd turned herself into a ruffian—*Guess that shows you, Harold.* In three days Vallie had come a long way, not just in miles.

Vallie held her breath until the trainman left and slammed the door behind him, leaving the baggage car in dusty darkness. Within minutes, wheels creaked and the train jerked forward. As her eyes got used to the dim light, she began to pick out shapes and shadows. High up on one side of the car, tiny lines of light showed. She dragged a trunk over and stood on it, reaching up as high as she could. She felt a handle and pulled, letting in light and fresh air. If she stood on tiptoe, she could see the countryside speed past.

I'll make myself a spot by the window, she decided, remembering how Grumpy Woman had stolen her first bench seat. *I'll show you, lady, and I'll show you yard bulls too.*

She stacked a second trunk atop the first so that she could sit and peek out the tiny window, closing it only when the train slowed for a station. Hour after hour Nebraska stretched as flat and green as the blotter on Uncle Franklin's desk, and after a while even looking out the window grew tiresome.

Night had fallen by the time the train finally pulled

into a big town. Vallie guessed it must be Denver because of all the lights. She scurried from her perch as the train's whistle blew and the wheels slowed. Yanking hard on the baggage car's door, she opened it and stepped out into the dark, windy space between the cars. Lights loomed ahead. *That must be the depot,* she guessed.

With her satchel tight in her hand, she counted, *One, two, three* . . . and jumped.

11

The End of the Line

Vallie landed hard on the cinder-covered ground, scraping her right knee. She stood, babying the leg for a moment, then, shifted her weight. It hurt, but she could walk.

I have to be extra careful here, she realized. Denver was the most dangerous place. Uncle Franklin would have men looking for her on every track.

Without her box, she felt light, moving through the shadows toward the depot. Soon she caught up to the arriving passengers and joined the throng hurrying to the main waiting room. Nobody stopped her—she prayed her luck would hold.

When she spotted the ticket seller's booth, she stepped into line. *I'm getting good at being a boy,* she realized as she swaggered up to the booth and grinned at the man who sat on a high stool behind the counter.

"Coach ticket to the mining camp in Aspen, please."

The man shook his head. "Sorry, boy. Ain't no such thing."

"Pardon?" Her smile slid right off her face.

"Trains don't run to Aspen. Track ain't built that far yet. I can get you to Leadville, about seventy miles from Aspen. That's the end of the line."

"Then what?" Vallie asked, trying to keep her voice from shaking.

"Then you're on your own."

Vallie sank into a seat, her confidence gone. She was on her own, all right. Even the long days and nights on the train hadn't felt as terrible as this moment. She dug into her satchel and counted up her belongings. One thick jacket, one sweater, a spare set of clothes, an empty milk bottle, plus seventeen dollars and sixty-five cents. It wouldn't carry her back to Pennsylvania, but it might take her to Leadville, wherever that was. *Oh, Papa, you'd better have full pockets when I find you.*

With a sigh, she stepped back into the line and bought a ticket, using up twelve-fifty. She spent another dollar on food for the trip. That didn't leave much to find a way from Leadville to Aspen, but she'd have to think about that later. The early-morning train boarded in half an hour, and Vallie decided to take it. She didn't want to wait around long enough to change her mind. It would be so easy to march up to a yard bull and tell him who she was. She shook her head firmly. *No, I will not go back!*

The Leadville train was mostly freight, it didn't carry many people. The passenger car was hitched right behind the coal cars, so more cinders and smoke blew in. Even if Vallie hadn't been grimy before, this train ride would have left her covered in soot. As they pulled out of Denver, she could finally see the mountains, a haze of purple far in the distance. But strangely, they were traveling in the opposite direction—away from the mountains and toward the rising sun.

"Excuse me," she said to the conductor who took her ticket. "Are we going to Leadville? I thought Leadville was west. This train seems to be traveling east."

The man grinned. "Sometimes you got to go east to get west. This here route's complicated. Sit tight, boy, and you'll get where you're going."

"I don't understand. How can you get west by going east?"

He chuckled. "Greenhorn. Train track runs through the passes. So first, we head for the right passes. Keep watching. You'll catch on."

As the day wore on, Vallie felt as if she needed a map to catch on. The train rolled south to Colorado Springs, then west for a while to Salida. It took forever—no wonder the ticket cost so much. When they finally reached the mountains, the air chilled and they hitched another engine on the front for more power.

Vallie's ears popped as the train rattled and creaked up the tracks and twisted through narrow places between red and gold cliffs. Papa was right, Colorado was beautiful, Vallie realized, but it was so big. She'd been traveling all day and still no sign of Leadville. "Hurry," she whispered to the engines. But they simply huffed along, straining to pull the heavy cars through rough terrain.

Darkness came and still the wheels churned. They rounded curve after curve, climbing the high passes, and then finally, in the distance, lights. As they drew closer, the city of Leadville shone in soft reds and browns, the buildings and dusty streets lit by gas lamps.

When the train pulled into the depot, Vallie took a deep breath. The end of the railroad line, and she had no notion how to get herself farther into these mountains, nor even where she might spend the night.

She climbed down the stairs, holding her satchel so tight her fingernails bit into her palm. *Brrr, it's cold.* And so high and mountainous and far from home—Leadville felt to Vallie like the very top of the world. But all that distance was a good thing, she told herself firmly. She'd come so far in her five long days of traveling, surely she'd left those Pinkertons behind.

Even though it was late, people still milled around the depot. A porter pulled carts for baggage, and she stepped up to him. "Please, sir. I want to travel to Aspen. How can I get there?"

"Stagecoach," the man replied.

"How much does it cost?"

"Twenty dollars or so."

"But . . ." She could barely catch a breath. "It's only seventy miles. How can it cost so much?"

"It's the only way in, unless you want to walk. Or take a jack train."

"What's a jack train? How much does that cost?"

"Jacks are mules. Cost depends if you ride or walk. How much you got?"

"Four dollars."

The man shrugged. "Head over to Bo Reston's stables. He might let you tag along."

"Where would I find the stables, please?"

"Far end of Main Street, past the big hotel." He pointed.

Vallie nodded and began to walk in the direction he'd suggested. At least there was a hotel in town. Maybe she'd splurge and rent a room. She could take a bath for the first time in nearly a week. She lifted her shoulders, cheered by the thought.

As she looked around, Leadville seemed to come to life. Even at night, men strode up and down the street, music poured out of open doors, lights shone at windows. Here she was, little Valentine Harper from Allegheny City, Pennsylvania, on her own in the wild, wild West. Her first impulse was to twirl in a circle, but boys didn't behave like that, so she smacked her knee instead.

A striped awning and fancy lettering decorated the front of a building across the street—the Clarendon Hotel. She crossed over and stepped inside. In the lobby, dark blue carpets cushioned her shoes. Gaslights burned along the walls, a grand staircase rose to a landing and a polished wooden counter welcomed travelers. She stepped up to the counter. "How much for a room, please?"

A young man wearing a satin vest frowned at her. "Dollar and a half, if we had any rooms free. You're too late, boy. Sorry." He didn't look sorry, though, Vallie thought.

A man and a woman paraded down the staircase. She wore a dark green silk dress, fancier than any Aunt Margaret owned. The man's suit was black and he wore gold rings on both hands. "Best move along, boy," the man behind the counter said.

Suddenly Vallie realized how rumpled and dirty she must look. Even if she'd taken the time to wash and change into the spare clothes in her satchel, they wouldn't have found a room for her. And the cost.

A dollar and a half. She'd need that for the mule train.

So I don't get a bath or a bed, she thought. *I'll find a bench and wait out the night.* With a sigh she left the hotel and turned toward the far end of the street and the mule stables.

Then she stopped stock-still. That man had just called her *boy,* and here she was, thinking like a girl. She didn't have to look clean or stay in a hotel. No, a boy could do what he wanted—sleep out under the stars, stay up all night, watch the sun rise.

Ahead, gaslight and loud voices spilled out of an open doorway. A gold-lettered sign hung above: HARRY'S SALOON.

Vallie sucked in a deep breath and puffed out her chest. A boy could even walk into a saloon if he wanted to. *And this boy wants to,* she decided, grinning and stepping closer. As she reached the doorway two men stumbled out, slugging away at each other.

Vallie crouched back, trying to fade into the shadows.

The men grunted and swore at each other. One fell down, and the other jumped on top of him, still punching.

Vallie pushed herself back farther until she could feel solid wood behind her.

As she watched, a third man ran to the pair on the ground. "Break it up now, break it up." He yanked on the collar of the man who was doing the pounding, dragging him away. The man on the ground sat up and rubbed one hand over his face.

Vallie's body trembled all over. She held out her right hand, the one she'd pounded Dirty Eddie with back in Omaha, and slowly curled it into a fist. That hadn't been a real fight, just one punch to chase off a bully. And he'd been small. These men were big. If one of them took a notion to pound on her, she couldn't do a thing to stop him. Even playing a boy wouldn't protect her.

She stood frozen against the building until all the men had gone. Then, keeping to the shadows, she crept along the street. Near the end, the warm smell of animals welcomed her. The stable was dark and she didn't see a soul, but there was a porch.

She climbed the steps and stood there, considering her choices. The rough porch wasn't much, but it had a roof and sides. That fight had shaken her up some. She didn't know what a real boy might do, but a girl wouldn't dare fall asleep in such a dangerous town.

She rubbed one hand along the splintery wood of the railing, trying to decide. She'd just have to stay awake all night, she figured. If she put on her sweater and the jacket from Joseph and Patrick, she wouldn't freeze. And tomorrow, she'd be right here, so when the mule train left, she'd be on it.

Vallie sank to the hard wooden floor of the porch and leaned back against the wall. Sounds drifted in the cold mountain air—piano music, people singing, a burst of laughter. Leadville was a busy, bustling city. Up and down the street people were having a good time with their friends. Except for Vallie. Wild West or not, she was cold, tired and nearly out of money. And she was alone.

12

Independence

Something wet hit Vallie's cheek. She opened her eyes and found herself staring into the muzzle of a large, shaggy brown dog. She shrank back against the porch railing.

Beyond the porch, Leadville looked odd in the early-morning light. Fancy buildings of wood, brick and stone faced stained, saggy, brown canvas tents. Small, rough cabins crowded the backstreets. Dust lay everywhere, and the air rang with the noise of machines, even early in the day. *Must be the silver mines,* Vallie guessed.

The dog thumped his tail and licked her again.

"Now then, Goliath, what have you found?"

Vallie jumped to her feet and came face-to-face with a big, bald-headed man. "Sorry. I didn't mean to clutter up your porch, but I arrived late last night on the train, and the hotel was full and these men were fighting and . . ." She spoke so fast, she had to stop and catch her breath.

"Settle down, boy. Settle down." The man smiled. She wasn't sure if he was settling her or the dog. "My name's Bo Reston. You looking for work, son? Plenty of jobs to be had in Leadville, that's for sure."

"No, sir. I'm trying to get to Aspen. My father's there."

"Come inside, this here dog's hungry."

Vallie sniffed. Even the dog had somebody to look after him. She cut off those pitiful thoughts quickly and followed Bo Reston and his dog inside to a small office. Reaching into her pocket, she asked, "How much is the jack train, please?"

"Riding's ten dollars."

Her fingers curled around the few coins she had left. "I don't have ten dollars."

"You're walking, then, I'd say. No charge for that. Save your money for grub and a bed on the trip."

"Walking?" Vallie had never walked from Allegheny to Pittsburgh—and that was just across a river bridge. How could she climb seventy miles in the Rocky Mountains? "How long does it take?"

"Three, four days. Depends on the weather. Might find you a better pair of boots, though. It's quite a climb."

"Boots?" Vallie shut her eyes. She couldn't afford boots, not if she wanted to eat.

"What's the matter, boy? You look like somebody

just shot your dog." As the man said "dog," the shaggy brown brute flopped near Vallie's feet and rolled onto his back, waving his paws in the air.

"I . . . I don't have money for boots," she said. "I used it for the train. I'm not sure I have enough for food. Or a place to sleep."

Don't break down, she told herself sternly. *You've come all this way, you can't puddle up now.* She thought of how close she was to finding Papa and squared her shoulders.

The big man looked her over as if she were a mule, then nodded. "I got a big load, I suppose I could use some help. Give me a hand with the jacks, you can come. Sleep in the haylofts along the way if you've a mind to."

"Yes. That would be fine."

He lifted a tin bucket. "I suppose you know how to hitch up?"

Vallie frowned. "No, sir. I don't. But I can haul water."

He passed her the bucket. "That's a start, I guess."

When the water trough was full, Bo Reston showed Vallie how to put on the mules' halters. After the first couple, she figured out which strap threaded through which buckle. The jacks didn't take too kindly to a stranger hitching them up and turned their heads away when she tried to loop the halter around their ears.

By the time she'd finished with ten halters, Bo had strapped packsaddles onto the backs of most of the animals and begun loading. Vallie carried heavy grain sacks from a wagon while he hefted them onto the mules. With every sack, her arms felt stretched and her back ached, but a boy wouldn't gripe, not to a big imposing man like Bo Reston, so Vallie swallowed her complaints.

Finally, when the wagon bed lay bare and all ten mules were loaded, he hitched the animals together.

"Mind if I wash up, sir?" Vallie asked. She hadn't minded grime on the train, but she was completely covered with dust and bits of hay and she smelled more like a mule than a girl. She'd dare any of those Pinkerton detectives to recognize her right this minute. Of course she'd left that worry far behind her in Denver. Thank heavens.

"Suit yourself." Bo Reston shook his head and grinned as if he knew something she didn't.

Vallie dunked her head into a pail of clean, cold water.

"We'll be heading out in five minutes," he warned. "And I don't take to no dawdling."

"Yes, sir." She shook water from her hair and ran for the privy. No chance for breakfast, but she had an apple left. She'd eat as she walked.

"I'm ready, sir," she said, slipping her satchel over one shoulder.

Bo Reston took it from her. "Here. Strap it on Old Bones."

"Thanks. I'll walk easier," she said.

"I doubt that," the man said, tying down her satchel. "If you stick with us all the way across Independence Pass, you'll have the hardest walk of your life. Don't say I didn't warn you."

"Yes, sir. I'm strong, sir." She wouldn't quit now, couldn't.

"You'd better be," he said.

It didn't take more than a mile for Vallie to understand why washing up had made the man smile. He stationed her at the end of the jack train where the mules' hooves raised a dusty cloud that surrounded her and made her throat sting. She had a handkerchief in her pocket, wrapped around her few remaining coins. She emptied it of money and tied it around her nose and mouth to keep out the worst of the dust. Would it really take four days to reach Aspen?

Four days later, she was making her way down a steep gravel trail, staring at the backside of Old Bones, the most cantankerous creature she'd ever met. She took in a dusty breath. The air was so thin and cold up here, it stung. She'd spent four days walking from morning until night, behind stubborn, stinking jacks, with bruises to prove it, and a sore, bone-tired body.

First they'd climbed up the pass, so the backs of Vallie's legs had burned—up into rocky cliffs and crumbling tracks, and finally up into deep dirty snow. Then down the pass, slipping and sliding and freezing.

Vallie examined her feet. Even the rags Bo Reston had given her to wrap inside her shoes didn't help. The leather was thick with dampness, stretched out of shape, and inside, the skin of her feet had blistered. Still, they were nearing Aspen.

Without warning, Old Bones jerked to a stop. Vallie caught herself and stepped off to one side, refusing to get into range of the mule's sharp hooves.

"Get up, you dumb mule, get up," she shouted.

Old Bones looked over his shoulder and stood stock-still. Bo Reston climbed up the trail to where Vallie and the mule stood. Goliath, the big dog, followed along, nosing the trail.

"What's the trouble, boy?"

"Old Bones again. He won't budge."

Reston tugged on the mule's harness. "I suppose he's tired. We've had quite a walk."

"Yep," she mumbled. *Quite a walk indeed.*

"How about you, boy?" the man asked. "Sun's going down, but we can make town if we push. You got another five miles in you?"

Vallie closed her eyes and imagined it. Aspen and Papa in just five more miles. What was five miles compared to the sixty-five they'd already covered? How much trouble was five miles downhill, after crossing the spine of the mountains, the continental divide . . .

"Sure, let's push on," Vallie said. "I got another five miles, easy."

"That's the spirit, boy. You ain't big, but you got grit." Bo grinned and slapped Old Bones on the rump.

It wasn't easy, though. It took every bit of strength Vallie had left and then some, to keep her sore feet moving down the pass. Independence, this pass was called, named by the miners when they'd found gold at the top on the Fourth of July.

Independent, that's what I am, Vallie kept telling herself as she trudged forward. *I made this trip on my own.* But as night came on and she huddled into the warm jacket Joseph and Patrick had given her, as she made out Bo Reston's shadowy bulk at the front end of the mule train, she realized she'd had lots of help.

Old Bones stopped again, and Vallie was tempted to kick out at the mule as he'd done to her so often. Then around a curve in the trail, she saw houses with lamps shining from the windows. They'd made town! Even Old Bones seemed to know, for after a brief pause, he plodded forward a bit faster than usual.

Vallie didn't need instructions when they arrived at the mule stables. By now she knew how to unload and unhitch and brush down the animals, knew how to lug sacks of grain and hoist them out of harm's way.

Bo Reston worked right beside her as they finished tending the jacks. "Pretty late to go looking for your pa," he said. "It's nearly midnight and decent folks will be abed by now."

"Yes, sir," Vallie replied, giving a final pat to the rump of a gray mule called Varmint.

"Got a hayloft here if you want to bed down." He tossed her a sack. "Some grub, if you're hungry. You earned it."

"Thanks."

Vallie found the water barrel and dipped some out to rinse her face and hands, then climbed the rough ladder to the hayloft. She was too tired to eat, almost too tired to dig herself a nest in the fragrant hay. Still, something drew her to the loft window. She unlatched it and stood, looking out. Aspen—Papa's town. At long last she'd arrived, and tomorrow her troubles would be over.

Small squares of brightness still shone from one or two windows, and at the far end of the town she could just make out the shadowy form of a tall, dark mountain. As she watched, pinpoints of flickering light appeared high up on the slope and began to move downward in a wavering line, like so many fireflies on parade. *Those lights look like stars,* Vallie thought, *for surely, I've landed in heaven.*

13

Aspen

Aspen didn't look quite so heavenly by the cold light of morning. Small cottages crowded the area around the stable, with a few canvas tents mixed in. The streets weren't streets at all, just hard-packed dirt with ruts. At the end of town, a mountain loomed, huge and brown.

Bo Reston directed her to the post office. "Best place to start looking," he said. "Postmaster knows who's who in this town."

Vallie washed herself as best she could, in a bucket of cold water, and put on her clean set of boy clothes from the satchel. A hot tub bath would sure have felt good, but at least she'd meet Papa clean.

On the way to the post office clumps of men in rough clothing walked past her toward the mountain carrying tin pails. Minutes later, another troop of men passed, tired and grimy, walking away from the mountain with their pails. Vallie wondered why they were so dirty already, but there wasn't anybody to ask.

Burly men crowded around the post office, so she could barely see the doorway. Vallie wanted to rush right up to the desk, but found herself at the end of a long line. *If they were more polite in this town,* she thought, *they'd let me go first.*

A glance at her filthy boots made her realize how foolish she was, and she almost laughed out loud. In those men's eyes she was rough too. They had no notion that she was a girl. She tried to curb her impatience. Finally she stood face-to-face with the postmaster and took a deep breath. "Please, sir. I'm looking for my father. His name is Daniel Harper and Bo Reston from the jack train said you'd know how to find him."

"Harper?" The man squinted. "Can't say I remember him. Name sounds familiar, though. Just a minute." He went back to a desk and sorted through a pile of envelopes, then returned with one, smiling.

"I thought so. There's a letter for him, just arrived. Daniel Harper. What did you say your name was?"

"I'm Valentine." Vallie lowered her voice. Even here, miles from Uncle Franklin, she didn't want to give herself away, not until she found her father. "Please, sir, Daniel Harper's my pa."

The postmaster passed her the envelope. "I might as well give you this, then. Pass it along to him when you find him."

His words felt as sharp as knives. Vallie gripped the envelope, mashing it in her hand without looking at it. "But sir. My father's been here in Aspen more than a year. Surely you know him. I've come a long way."

The man shook his head sadly. "You know how many men have passed through this town in the last year? Between miners, prospectors, greenhorns and drifters, must be thousands. Sorry, boy. I don't know your pa. Try the saloons."

"But . . ." Vallie's throat went dry. She stepped away from the counter and fumbled toward the door. Outside, she leaned against the side of the post office so that she wouldn't topple over. Her heart pounded away in her chest like a crazy drum. She wanted to shout at the postmaster and *make* him find Papa, but the man couldn't help. Nobody could help, and it made Vallie fuming mad. She was here, in Aspen, Papa was here too. But he was no saloon man, so how was she supposed to find him?

She looked down. In her hand she still clutched the letter. *Here I am fussing and I haven't even checked the letter. There will be news here, there has to be. . . .* She tore open the envelope and unfolded the single page.

The familiar handwriting mocked her—*Dear Papa, School is nearly done and* . . . No! It was *her* letter. She crumpled the paper into a ball and stuffed it into her pocket. A salty taste gathered at the back of her throat. She sniffed, trying to hold in the tears that threatened to pour out.

She looked up and down the street. Such a big town—shops and businesses and houses. Thousands of men had passed through, leaving their footprints in the dust. Finding one among so many was impossible.

She'd come all this way by herself, and she'd failed. Now she was stuck in Aspen, with no chance of finding her father and only enough money to buy a single day's worth of food.

I'll have to go back to Pennsylvania, she thought. *But I can't do that either, not on the single dollar I've got in my pocket.*

Rubbing her sleeve against her damp cheeks, she slumped onto a set of dusty steps and ran her fingers across the rough splintery wood. As she sat there, the tears dripped, darkening the wood, and she gave up trying to hide them. She was more than a thousand miles from home and all alone. A girl deserved a good cry about that.

A creaking of wheels and a clop-clop of hooves made her look up. Bo Reston had pulled his wagon to a stop. "Bad news, son?"

She swiped at her eyes. "No news at all. Postmaster doesn't know my father."

The mule driver swung down from the wagon seat,

still holding the reins. "Sorry to hear that, Vallie. What you going to do?"

"I don't know. I'm out of money and out of luck."

"Can't say as you can change your luck." The man rubbed his bald head as if thinking. "But you could earn yourself some money. You ain't afraid of hard work."

"No, sir." It was all Vallie could do to reply politely; she wanted to hide away somewhere and just cry.

"Well, boy, I'm betting you can't walk up one side of Cooper Avenue and down the other without seeing at least one sign."

"Sign? I don't understand."

The big man shook his head. "Look around you. Place is booming. Miners working three shifts, around the clock. They keep the cafés and boardinghouses busy. Somebody's always looking for help."

"You mean a job?" Vallie swallowed. "How . . . how would I find a place that needed help?"

"Like I said, walk along Cooper—lots of restaurants there. Look for notices in the windows." He pointed.

Some of the heaviness that had settled around her lifted. She nodded. "Thanks, Mr. Reston, sir. I sure appreciate your help."

"Good luck to you, son. Now I got some deliveries to make down the river a piece, but I should get back partway through the afternoon. You stop by the stable and let me know what's what, hear?"

"Yes, sir. Thanks again."

She stepped into the dusty street and crossed over toward Cooper Avenue. As she turned down the street, she waved at Bo Reston.

He saluted her and his wagon wheels began to roll.

14

The Silver Dollar

I can do this. I can find a job.

Head high, shoulders back, Vallie marched along the hard dirt street, close to the wooden buildings. Something sharp bit into the sole of her foot. She bent to get it out and shook her head at the sorry condition of her shoes. Near the toe of her right oxford, the leather had rotted and ripped away from the sole. She kicked out a stone and kept walking, peering in every window.

She passed two hotels, a barbershop and a stationery shop, four saloons, a restaurant and a jeweler. Then on the corner, she spotted a café, with a sign in the window: BOY WANTED.

Vallie hesitated. A café wasn't as bad as a saloon, but it was bad enough. Back in Allegheny City, she and Aunt Margaret had occasionally visited a tearoom wearing their best dresses, hats and gloves. But Vallie had never before stepped inside a rough-looking eating place and she doubted her aunt had either.

Aunt Margaret would faint dead away at the thought of Vallie's going inside, but then Aunt Margaret was probably having palpitations of the heart by now anyway. What would Bridget think? Or Papa? Surely they'd want her to eat, and where better than a café?

She took a deep breath, pushed open the door and walked over to a wooden counter. A tall, pale woman stood behind it, drying glasses. She wore an apron over a dark blue dress and her light braids were coiled around her head like a crown. "What'll it be?"

"Your sign," Vallie began. "You're wanting a boy for work?"

The woman tossed down her towel. "Last boy went off to work in the mines and I need help." She stepped from behind the counter and took a hard look at Vallie. "This isn't just any old cookhouse, you understand. I have standards." She pointed to a sign.

THIS IS A DECENT ESTABLISHMENT!

NO POKER PLAYING • NO DICE THROWING
NO GAMBLING WHATSOEVER

NO SPITTING ON THE FLOOR • NO FISTFIGHTS

IF YOU SMELL TOO MUCH LIKE YOUR MULE,
TAKE A BATH BEFORE YOU EAT.

The last notice made Vallie grin. Good thing she'd washed this morning. And she was decent—she didn't do any of the things mentioned on the notice.

"You a hard worker?"

"Yes, ma'am. I just came over the pass with Mr. Bo Reston. Helped with his mules. I'd rather wash glasses. What's the pay?"

"Fifty cents a day and found. Sundays off—not like those other heathenish places."

"Found?"

"Meals. A bed if you need one, shed off the kitchen."

"I could use a bed," Vallie said.

"Breakfast too, I'll warrant. I'm Nora Jensen. My husband and I own the Silver Dollar Café." The woman stuck out her hand and Vallie shook it.

"Vallie Harper. When could I start, Mrs. Jensen?"

"You call me Nora, now. How about starting after breakfast?"

Nora showed Vallie to an unpainted room off the kitchen with barely enough space for a small cot and a washstand. Hooks lined up along the back of the door for clothes. A small towel hung from one. Vallie set her satchel on the table. She ran her hand across the woolen blanket and its roughness caught her skin, but a bed was better than a loft and the sheets looked clean.

"My husband, Peter, and I live upstairs," Nora

explained. She steered Vallie back to the kitchen and set a heaping plate of food on a table.

"I'll work you hard, but there's no better cook in Aspen. Now, here's how the place runs. We get three shifts of miners—eight in the morning, four in the afternoon, and midnight. That's three big meals to cook every day."

Vallie scuffed her toe along the plank floor. "I can't cook, ma'am. Never learned how."

"Nobody's expecting that from a boy like you. Your job is to serve, and wash up after every meal. When that's done, you can spend your time as you like."

"That's real nice of you, ma'am," Vallie said. "This seems like a good place to work."

Nora nodded and pointed to the sign. "It's as good as I can make it, in a rough town like this. We get the same fellas, eating before work and again after. And they know my rules. I won't put up with any nonsense." She frowned at Vallie. "Where'd you come from, boy?"

"Back East. I'm looking for my father. He came here to find his fortune in silver."

"Him and a thousand others," Nora grumbled.

"Do you know him? His name's Daniel Harper?"

"Sorry, can't say I've heard the name, but ask the miners. One of them might know something. And Vallie . . ."

"Yes, ma'am?"

"Got any money in your pocket?"

"Not much."

Nora reached into her apron. "Here's two bits, then. Advance on today's pay. Get yourself to the barbershop. I run a decent place, I don't employ ragamuffins."

"Yes, ma'am." A barber would cut her hair even shorter. But if she wanted to eat, she needed a job. Nora seemed decent and strict—even Aunt Margaret would like that. Vallie could be safe with a roof over her head and hot meals if she worked for Nora and looked for Papa. Surely he'd understand.

As she walked to the barbershop, a little boy rode past in a cart pulled by a large black dog. School here must be finished for the year, Vallie realized, and it would be over back in Allegheny too. The last day, when she should have been wearing her best dress and celebrating, had passed. Instead of hugging her classmates goodbye, she'd been following a string of stubborn mules down a snowy mountain pass.

"Just a trim, please." She sat, stiff and nervous, in the shiny red barber chair.

The barber made quick work of her hair, snipping away curls until her head felt dizzy. In the mirror, her face looked lean, her chin pointy. A skinny boy, with a short, short haircut. There wasn't much of the old Valentine left.

As Vallie left the shop, she almost cried. If she'd known how hard it would be to find her father, she might have thought twice before traveling across the country alone. But before she could feel too bad about her situation, she scolded herself. *I'm not some sissy, afraid to get my hands dirty,* she thought. *I avoided Pinkertons and yard bulls. I climbed right across the Continental Divide in knee-deep snow with Bo Reston and his mules and I found a job and a place to stay. So I* will *find Papa! It's just a matter of time.*

She'd start searching as soon as she got herself settled in at the café. The sooner she found her father, the sooner she could return to the old Vallie. She brushed her hand against the back of her head and felt the short, bristly hair. Well, not the old Vallie, she decided, but at least she could turn back into a girl. How long did it take hair to grow, anyhow?

Vallie stopped in the mercantile on her way back to the Silver Dollar. She needed new shoes, or better, boots. An ordinary pair of boy's socks would be nice too, so she wouldn't have to wrestle with her long girl's stockings under her trousers.

As she entered the shop, a girl about her age was leaving with her mother. The girl wore a fancy white dress with ruffles on the skirt, and her hair was done up in ringlets. Vallie smiled, but the girl didn't smile back.

How annoying, Vallie thought, until she realized this girl couldn't see beyond her disguise. Back at home, Vallie herself didn't smile at strange-looking, rough boys either. Still, being ignored made her feel lonely. Back in Omaha, Joseph and Patrick had looked plenty grimy, but they'd been kind.

"May I help you?" The shopkeeper stood behind a wooden counter. Behind him, shelves overflowed with bolts of cloth, making Vallie's eyes hungry for calicoes and soft, pale linens. A ruffled parasol caught her eye, but she resisted it. What in the world would a boy do with such frippery? But when she found her father and turned back into herself . . . The man cleared his throat.

She'd been dawdling and he was busy. "Well now, boy, can't I interest you in a nice pair of suspenders? Right snappy!" He chuckled.

"No, thanks anyway." Suspenders! Wait till she came back to buy that parasol. His eyes would pop. For now, she needed her practical shoes.

"I need boots, sir, if they're not too dear."

"What size?"

"I'm not sure." She sat on a bench across from the counter and took off one of her oxfords. It barely looked like a shoe. She wished she didn't have to show it to the man, but he needed to figure her size. "I came through the pass," she explained.

"Wearing these? I'd say they're about used up." He bustled around and returned with two pairs of sturdy brown lace-up boots. "One pair of these should fit. Give them a try."

The first pair pinched Vallie's toes, but the second slid on and felt just right. She tightened the laces and tried walking around. "How much, sir?"

"That'd be a dollar, son."

Vallie sighed. Her last dollar. But she couldn't very well walk around Aspen barefoot. "All right. I need socks too. I'll come back when I get paid."

"I'll throw in a pair of socks. New boots deserve new socks." He smiled and tossed her a pair of thick cotton ones.

She had the feeling he was giving her a bargain, and not just on the socks. "Thanks a lot."

She scurried from the mercantile to Bo Reston's stables to tell him about her job. When she pounded on the door, nobody answered.

"Reston's gone off in his wagon," called a man sitting on the porch of the cottage next door. "Can I help you?"

"Thanks," Vallie said. "Please tell him that Vallie got a job at the Silver Dollar Café. I'd be obliged."

"Sure thing. Silver Dollar Café. I got that." The man pointed to his head and nodded as if he'd somehow written it all down in his mind.

Back at the Silver Dollar, Nora studied Vallie's haircut. "You look decent," she said. "How about giving me a hand with the morning's dishes?"

"Yes, ma'am."

Vallie hauled water and heated it for scrubbing dishes. Then she scoured out pots and skillets. She wiped down all the café tables and swept the floor. While she worked, Nora soaked beans and peeled potatoes. She mixed up bread dough and set it to rise.

"Where's Mr. Jensen?" Vallie asked when she'd finished the scrubbing.

"He'll be along. Doesn't spend much time here during the day. He runs a land office, as well as the café. He'll make his fortune without all that filthy digging. There's more than one way to get rich in a town like Aspen."

The word *filthy* caught Vallie's attention. "Nora? Would I be allowed a bath, please? When my chores are done?"

"You know how to heat water, don't you? Tub's in the back."

Later, as she sat surrounded by the hot water in the copper bathtub, Vallie thought over what she'd learned from Nora. She hoped Papa was getting rich too, so that when she found him, she wouldn't have to wash dishes three times a day. Her fingers had turned to prunes.

Still, she was grateful for the free bath. She sank down in the hot water and counted back—four days on the jack train, four or five on the railroad. Eight or nine days since she'd taken a real bath. And this was the first time she'd ever heated her own water. "You'd be proud of me, Papa," she said softly. "I'm taking care of myself."

Papa—Vallie's eyes filled. Only a few hours ago she'd expected to find him through the post office, and already she had a job, a haircut and new boots. It didn't seem possible, yet the tired aching in her legs proved how hard she'd worked.

Remembering the way the girl with the ringlets had stared right through her, Vallie scrubbed at her short, ugly hair with a bar of strong brown soap. The suds stung her eyes and this time she let hot tears roll into the bathtub. She couldn't help feeling sorry for herself—she looked so terrible now that nobody, not even Papa, would recognize her. The real Valentine Harper had gotten lost along with her clothes, somewhere between Allegheny and Aspen. The person in the bathtub didn't know how to bring her back.

And worse, not a single soul had recognized Papa's name. Vallie had a terrible feeling that he'd gotten lost too, swallowed up by the huge, harsh mountains. She didn't have the slightest notion of how to find him either.

15

Strays

"So you're the new boy. Welcome to Aspen and the Silver Dollar." Peter Jensen's voice boomed out. His ruddy cheeks and wide smile made Vallie smile right back in spite of herself.

"Thank you, sir." It was three in the afternoon, nearly time for the before-work miners to trickle in for a meal. Vallie had tried to leave her worries behind with the dirty bathwater.

"Where'd you come from? What are your plans?" Peter stood behind the bar, setting out glasses.

"Came from back East," Vallie said. "I'm looking for my father. You wouldn't know a Daniel Harper, would you?"

"Nope. What's he do here?"

"He's looking for silver," Vallie said.

"You must know more than that, boy. Is he a miner? Prospector? Investor?"

"I'm not sure. Back home he used to teach science in the high school. Geology was his favorite. Now he's trying to discover veins of silver in these mountains. That's what he says in his letters."

"Prospector, then. They're the hardest to find. Man takes a couple of jacks, he can travel hundreds of miles in these mountains. He might not have a room in town. More likely, he'll carry a tent along and live rough."

Hundreds of miles? Peter Jensen's words turned Vallie's stomach to lead. "How would I find him, then?"

"I wouldn't try. Better off looking for his mines."

"Pardon?"

"Look for his mines. Get yourself over to the claims office. If he's found silver, he'll be in the mine claims book."

"Thanks, sir. Thanks a lot."

"And Valentine, I got another job for you, after supper's done with."

"I'll be glad to help. What do you need?"

The scuffing of boots sounded and the door opened. Vallie turned to see a line of men filing into the café and finding seats at tables.

"Go on, boy. Take care of the customers. We'll talk again once supper's over."

Vallie made trip after trip to the kitchen, returning with steaming plates. Some men wanted breakfast, for they were on their way to work. Others wanted supper. Nora had both prepared.

When Vallie could, she asked the men about her father, but they only seemed to know other miners who worked the same shift, or people who lived in the same rooming houses.

When the first group of men finished their wedges of dried-apple pie, Vallie hurried to clear the tables and scrub them clean for the next batch, who came in dirty and tired. They wanted supper and kept Peter plenty busy pouring beer for them to drink with their meals and whiskey afterward.

Vallie was clearing away the second set of plates when Bo Reston stepped inside the Silver Dollar with another man. They took seats at the bar and ordered mugs of beer.

"How are you doing, boy?" Bo asked when she'd returned from the kitchen with empty hands. "They treating you right?"

"Yes, sir. Thanks for asking."

"That Nora, she's a caution. But she'll treat you fair. Best cook in Aspen too. I eat here when I'm in town."

Vallie smiled. "Guess I'll serve you supper now and then."

"You will indeed." Bo Reston nodded toward the other man. "I'd like you to meet a friend of mine, Bramblet Willis. He's got a ranch downriver a ways, raises horses and mules. Buys grain from me. This here's Vallie Harper, Bram."

"Pleased to meet you," Vallie said. She studied Bramblet Willis. He was tall, like Bo Reston, with light brown hair and a full bristly beard.

"Any news of your pa?" Bo asked. "Told my friend here you were hunting him. I expect by now you've asked half the folks in town."

"I've asked some," Vallie admitted. "Mr. Jensen said I should try the claims office. Said if I found Papa's mines, I'd probably find Papa."

Bo nodded. "Good advice."

She turned to Bo's friend. "You wouldn't know a Daniel Harper, would you, Mr. Willis?"

"Bramblet, please. And no, I'm sorry, I don't know your pa." The man studied her carefully with serious-looking green eycs. It made Vallie feel as if she were a bug in a jar.

"Jensen's a smart man," Bramblet added. "But you'll have to wait till Monday. Claims office shuts down Saturdays and Sundays."

Monday—that meant wasting two whole days. Vallie tried to hide her disappointment with a smile.

A couple of hours later, when Peter was explaining the special job he had for her, Vallie couldn't even remember how to smile. Every muscle she owned ached, and her fingers stung from the strong soap she'd used for washing dishes.

She stood on the back stoop of the Silver Dollar while Peter nudged at a wooden crate with the pointed toe of his boot. “I’ll keep the mother,” he explained. “And one of the kittens. But you’ve got to get rid of the rest.”

In the box, five lively kittens tumbled and batted each other while their mother watched. Vallie’s fingers itched to play with them. “Get rid of?”

“That’s right. Can’t have six cats. Give them away if you can.”

“If I can’t?” Vallie wasn’t sure she wanted to hear the answer.

“Tie them in a sack with a good-sized rock and toss them in the river tomorrow night.”

“In the river. Yes, sir.” Vallie’s voice trembled. She could never do such a thing. “Could I have more time, sir? A week, to give them away?”

Peter frowned, then he shrugged. “All right, a week. This time next Friday, I want them gone, worthless strays. And Vallie . . .”

“Yes, sir?”

“About Nora. I’d like you to keep an eye out. She can act as tough as a jack mule, but . . .”

“But?”

“She’s had her share of trouble. Folks aren’t always what they seem, you see. So treat her kindly, keep your eyes open, all right?”

“Sure.” Vallie frowned, not sure what she was supposed to be watching for. But she’d do her best to behave well and be friendly.

Vallie woke early the next morning and got to work right away. As soon as the last plate was dried and the last pot scrubbed, she spoke to Nora. "Mind if I go out for a while?"

Nora wiped her hands on her apron. "Help yourself. The kitchen looks tidy. Here, seventy-five cents and we'll be square."

Vallie tossed the coins in her hand. Seemed as if she'd worked pretty hard for just three jangly quarters. Still, some money was better than none, and it was more than those little boys earned back in Omaha.

"Thanks." Vallie stuck the money into her pocket and hurried outdoors. She wondered how a person was supposed to survive on a couple of short spells of sleep instead of a whole night.

Don't be such a grump, she told herself. *Today's Saturday, and by this time Monday you'll find Papa and won't have to worry about such things.* Monday couldn't come soon enough.

With a deep sigh, she decided to explore more of the town and turned toward Hyman Avenue, which seemed to have the nicest shops. Cooper served mostly miners with eating places, saloons and tobacconists. She'd been warned by Nora to stay away from Durant Avenue, for it was rough and rowdy and wicked, so she only peered at that street from a distance.

On the way back to the Silver Dollar, her nose caught a sweet scent. She looked around and saw a sign—JULES BERG, CONFECTIONER. *Just what I need,* Vallie thought, something sweet. She spent a nickel on fudge, a few pennies on lemon drops, then fingered her remaining coins. They didn't add up to much, but she could buy stamps and paper. She plopped down on the steps of the confectioner's shop and popped a lemon drop into her mouth.

Time to write to Bridget, she decided. *But how will she get the letter?* Uncle Franklin picked up the family's mail at the post office. He'd be sure to examine a letter for Bridget and notice the Colorado postmark. Then he'd send some of those detectives out on the very next train to find Vallie. *So I can't write no matter how badly I want to. Forgive me again, Bridget.*

From up on the mountain the noon whistle blew, calling the miners to their midday meal. Vallie's stomach growled. Back at the Silver Dollar, she made a sandwich and headed for the back stoop. The wooden crate sat in a sunny corner, and inside, the mother cat lay stretched out with her five babies piled around her. As Vallie ate, she studied the kittens. Which one might she keep for the café? Perhaps the all-black boy kitten. She'd name him Pepper. She'd give away the rest this very afternoon; she couldn't even bring herself to imagine the other choice.

Vallie trudged the busy streets of Aspen offering folks the four remaining kittens, stopping at every shop and saloon's back door. "Want a kitten? They'll keep the mice away." And then, "Do you know Daniel Harper?"

Mostly people shook their heads. "Sorry. Have a cat already. Sorry, don't know any Harpers."

At the Windsor Hotel, she gave away a gray stripy kitten with big paws. The cook had smiled at her and stuck the little fellow right into her apron pocket. "A coyote made off with our last cat," the woman explained. "We could use a good mouser."

"And Daniel Harper? Do you know him? He's my father."

"Check at the front desk, boy," the cook advised. "They keep records."

Vallie spent half an hour reading a long list of names in the hotel's guest book, but no Daniel Harper showed up. "Thanks anyway," she said.

"Good luck, son," the desk man replied.

Vallie walked on, trying to give away the rest of the kittens.

She found a home for the other male with the man who ran the hardware store. "Got me a little girl at home, she's been pestering for a kitty. This little fella with the white patches looks real lively."

"He's a rascal, all right," Vallie agreed. "And sir, I know you're busy, but do you know my father? Daniel

Harper—he's looking for silver. I bet he bought supplies from you."

"Half the country buys supplies from me. Sorry, boy."

"Thanks anyway. Hope your little girl likes the cat." A cool wind blew down from the mountains as Vallie left the hardware store. Thinking about that nice man carrying home a kitten for his daughter made Vallie shiver. It had been so long since Papa had hugged Vallie or teased her, she had a hard time remembering how it felt. But her waiting was almost over.

She closed her eyes and tried to picture Monday morning at Papa's mine. She'd arrive dressed as a boy. She could even ask for a job at first, as a joke. Then she'd wait a minute or two, until Papa recognized her. *Valentine, heart of my heart,* he'd say. Then he'd lift her up and swing her in a circle the way he always did.

If she hadn't grown too tall, of course. And if he recognized her.

She sat on the hardware store's porch and lifted out the two remaining kittens. "It isn't easy being a stray, is it? But tomorrow I'll find you both good homes, just see if I don't. And on Monday it will be my turn."

16

Gravestones

That Saturday the early supper and midnight shifts brought more hungry miners into the Silver Dollar. But Sunday was a day of rest, and Vallie had earned it. She slept well into the morning and awakened only when Nora rapped on her door.

"Will you go to church with us, Vallie? We go to the Congregationalist services."

"Sure."

"Be ready in an hour," Nora said. "Breakfast's waiting in the kitchen."

Vallie washed herself carefully and tried to smooth her short hair with wet hands. To celebrate the day off, she put on the new pair of socks and clean clothes she'd rinsed out on Friday.

Still, it only took a few minutes to get ready. Quite a change from Sundays back at home, when Bridget curled her long hair and made sure each petticoat was fluffed out just right. And Vallie didn't have to wear a hat. Back in Allegheny, all the women and girls wore hats. She hoped God wouldn't mind that she didn't cover her head today, but even if she'd owned a cap, as a boy she'd have to snatch it off her head the minute she entered church.

At home she'd gone to the Presbyterian church, and she didn't want to make too many mistakes if the Congregationalists did things differently. But the services were so similar, Vallie found herself knowing when to stand up and when to sit without difficulty. She joined in the hymns and sang the words by heart. Nora took notice and smiled.

During the last hymn people sang about heaven as their final resting place, and although the tune felt joyful, Vallie had a hard time singing. Those words, *final resting place*, stuck in her head. *Papa? Is that why I haven't found him?* Her throat thickened. *I won't cry, I won't,* she told herself. She stiffened her back and took a deep breath.

After the last *amen,* she rushed out of the church. Outdoors, she stopped for a moment and stepped close to a woman wearing a large straw hat with pink roses circling the crown. "Please, ma'am. Could you direct me to the cemetery?"

"Walk toward Aspen Mountain, turn left at the last street. Meander on awhile and you'll come to it."

"Thank you." Vallie hurried from the churchyard,

where more and more people gathered to chew over the week's news. She strode toward the mountain, which stood guard, strong and dark, against the blue, blue sky.

Reaching the last street, she turned left as the woman had instructed and speeded her pace until she was running. The dirt street gave way to a grassy lane, and still Vallie ran. Her breath was coming hard and fast when she finally spotted a new iron fence with a fancy scrolled gate. The gate stopped her for a moment, and she tried to catch her breath.

The iron felt cool and smooth under her fingers, and the gate squeaked as she pushed it open, sending a chill up her back. Inside the fence, she saw a few stones and wooden slabs marking graves. Around the graves the meadow grass had been carefully clipped and tended. Wild iris grew in clumps alongside a bright blue flower she didn't recognize.

She checked each grave marker. A number were carved with small lambs and belonged to babies. Seeing them made Vallie sad. Then she caught sight of a familiar name—Nellie Jensen, b.d. September 1884, age two weeks. Vallie could almost hear Peter Jensen's voice in her ears, asking her to watch out for Nora. Now she knew why. Poor Nora, she was hauling a wagonload of sorrow—no wonder she had a sharp tongue sometimes. She swallowed hard and stepped quickly away from the child's grave.

Still, at each name, Vallie felt relief. It didn't seem as if Daniel Harper was resting here after all. Then the gate squeaked again and she looked up to see Nora, standing straight as a tree. Nora made it a point not to look at her baby's stone. Vallie followed her example.

"Vallie? Whatever are you doing? You ran from church like a rabbit. I thought you were sick."

"I'll be all right," Vallie said. She read the name on the newest stone and let out a long breath. "Is this the only graveyard in town?"

Nora nodded. "One's a plenty. Why?"

"Well, I didn't find Papa's name here. S-So that's good."

"Amen to that, boy. Let's get back to the Silver Dollar."

That afternoon, Vallie decided to try to give away the kittens in the nicer part of town. The hardware man had wanted a pet for his little girl, so maybe another family would feel the same way. Nora gave her directions to Bleeker Street, and she headed off. The two remaining kittens looked like their mother, with orangey fur. They were so sweet, Vallie was sure nobody could resist them.

The first family she approached was polite, but not terribly friendly. "No cats. We have dogs."

The next house had a teepee in the side yard. Two little girls about six or seven were playing with dolls in the teepee. They wore frilly dresses and had buggies for their dolls, and beds and chairs and all sorts of fancy toys. But when Vallie stepped toward the teepee, a stern woman strode out from the back of the house and scolded. "Move along. No rough boys wanted here."

"But I . . . What about kittens? They're very cute." She held out the basket.

The woman folded her arms across her chest and gave Vallie a cold stare. "I said move along."

"Yes, ma'am."

The next house was empty, and at the one after, two older people sat on the porch. Still Vallie tried. "Kittens? They'll keep the mice away."

"Are you suggesting that we have mice?" the woman asked. "Well, I never."

"Sorry, ma'am."

Vallie trudged along one side of Bleeker Street and crossed to the other. She saw girls her own age, who looked at her curiously but wouldn't say hello. She saw younger children, whose mothers kept them away from somebody as rough as Vallie.

Near the end of the street, she saw the dogcart she'd seen in town. The same little boy was steering while a man walked alongside. She held out her basket and said, "Interested? They're free."

"Oh, Papa, kittens. Let's look."

Vallie stepped closer; the dog that was pulling the

cart sniffed and lunged for the basket, dumping over the cart. The man grabbed the dog's collar and wrestled him down. "Sit, you big brute. Sit." Then he turned and lifted the little boy from the ground. One of the little boy's legs was strapped to a splint.

"Are you all right, Toby?"

"I'm fine, Papa. I guess Thunder doesn't like kittens, does he?"

Vallie backed away quickly. "Sorry. I didn't mean to upset your dog." When she came to a side street she took it, leaving Bleeker behind. Back on Main Street, she slumped on the top step of the newspaper office.

With shaking hands, she pulled the pale kittens into her lap and rubbed their small bellies. The kittens began to purr. "Nobody wants you, do they? They don't seem to think much of me either. But I'll find you homes."

Peter Jensen had called the kittens strays, but he could have called her that too. She closed her eyes and saw friendly faces, Joseph and Patrick from the train depot in Omaha. They were strays, but they'd been kinder than the fancy people on Bleeker Street. She looked down at the kittens. One was larger than the other, with a tip of white on her ear. "I'll call you Patsy," she said, scratching the ear. "And you're Josie, little one, for Joseph."

The kittens purred even more loudly. Their low rumbles soothed Vallie. "You like your names, do you? That's good. It's not every day a person gets to name new cats." She rubbed one silky kitten with each hand. "The boys in Omaha, they'd be pleased too. Even though you're girl cats. Wish they could meet you. It's just a darned shame my new friends are more than three hundred miles away."

Vallie shook her head, wishing things were different. If Papa were here, she could turn back into her own self and make real friends. She wouldn't have to spend a beautiful Sunday prowling graveyards and talking to cats.

17

A Rich Man

Monday morning Vallie stood at the kitchen sink. Today, today she'd find Papa. She scrubbed and scraped at top speed.

By ten she arrived at the claims office, where she spoke to a balding man sitting at a desk piled high with papers. "I'm looking for my father, sir. I was told that finding his mine might help." She was so anxious to start searching, it was hard to speak slowly and politely, but she tried.

The man turned and smiled. He wore spectacles, which he took off and polished as he spoke. "It might indeed. When did he come to Aspen? We've got books and books of claims."

Vallie looked around at the crowded shelves, overwhelmed. "Winter of 1884."

"Probably got out here and geared up in time for

the summer season, then. No prospecting goes on until the snow melts and the mud dries."

He reached up to a shelf and sorted through several books, then placed a tall stack on a nearby table. "That starts in May and goes through October of last year. Haven't had too much business yet this year, so you'd best read through those."

Vallie ran her fingers over the top book. "So many mines? I've never done this before, sir. How do I go about looking? Is it alphabetical?"

"No, the entries are by date." He flipped open the first book. "See here. Each entry has the name of the mine claim, names of the owners, date of discovery and general description. You'll just need to read through."

Vallie swallowed. The first entry took up most of a page and the writing was small. "Thanks. This could take a while. I'd better get to work." She sat in a straight-backed chair, bent over the table, and began to scan names.

The Caroline. The Last Chance. The Lucky Lady. Back Breaker. *What odd names for mines,* Vallie thought. And so many men had come here—Cornelius Popper, John Robert Morehead, Henry Denby. Soon the names of the prospectors and their mines blurred together.

By the time the noon whistle blew, Vallie had only studied half of the first ledger book and her eyes stung. The bald man smiled at her. "Any luck?"

She tried to rub the tiredness out of her eyes. Monday morning was gone and she'd barely started on the pile of books. "Not yet. The handwriting is so tiny, and some of it's messy."

"Prospectors come from all over. Some are educated men, but some can barely write their names."

In midafternoon, Vallie closed the first book and fought off a wave of disappointment. She hadn't found Papa's name anywhere from May through early June of 1884. But a year ago he'd been new to prospecting—he wasn't likely to find silver right away, she figured. She had to keep looking.

"I'll be back tomorrow, if it's all right."

"See you then. Good day, son."

After sitting indoors on that straight chair, Vallie enjoyed stretching her legs on the walk back to the Silver Dollar, with the sun warming her shoulders.

Too soon, it was time for work. "Shall I set the tables now, Nora?"

"Set them all, and then make sure the glasses behind the bar don't have any smudges. Hot as it is, we'll have a thirsty crew today, and I don't want to run out of clean glasses."

"Yes, ma'am." Vallie bustled around, getting ready for the afternoon shift to arrive. A few minutes before three, as she was polishing glasses, the café door opened and a very dirty man staggered in.

"Hallelujah!" he shouted. "Days of glory are coming! I found me the mother lode! Drinks for everyone."

Vallie looked around. Hadn't the man noticed that she was the only person in the room?

Nora rushed in from the kitchen. "Now see here," she began.

The man stepped toward Nora on unsteady feet, lifted her up and spun her around. "I'm a rich man. Won't you dance with me, girlie?"

"Put me down!" Nora wriggled free. "Vallie, give me a hand."

Vallie stepped closer, not sure what to do.

Nora grasped the man's right arm firmly. "This is a decent establishment, sir. We'll have none of your rambunctious behavior here. Vallie, take his other arm and help me escort him to the street."

"But I'm a rich man," he bellowed.

"You're also filthy, drunk and loud enough to wake snakes. We don't put up with such."

Between them, Nora and Vallie steered the man outside. Nora pointed up the street. "See there. Up at the hotel you can get a bath. Go on to Durant or Galena Street if you want to act rowdy. Vallie, you walk a ways with him, to make sure he doesn't come back."

Vallie swallowed hard. "Yes, ma'am." The man stank of sweat and liquor and Vallie didn't want to touch him. But she'd promised Peter she'd help Nora.

She dragged on one of his dirty arms and felt as if she needed a whole bath herself.

As the man staggered up the street, he shouted to everyone who passed by. "I'm a rich man! Found the mother lode! Let me buy you a drink!"

When he'd walked a full block, he turned to Vallie. "Girlie back at the café says I need a bath. What do you think, boy?"

His words jumbled in Vallie's ears. She wasn't sure if he was calling her a girlie, or if he meant Nora. She was too scared to answer.

"What do you think?" he repeated. "Do I stink? Do I need a bath?"

"Yes. You need two baths." Vallie tugged him toward the Windsor Hotel.

"Splendid. Two it is, then. You come along. Give you a silver nugget if you'll scrub my back and fetch me some dandy new duds."

"What?" Vallie shouted. Give a man a bath? A scandal like that and Aunt Margaret would call up the army. It was all Vallie could do not to laugh outright at the notion.

The man kept talking in a loud voice. "Yessir. You come along, son. Spruce me up right nice, and I'll make you my assistant. You can count up all my money. How about that?"

Vallie delivered him to the door of the Windsor Hotel and gave him a shove. "Sorry, mister, I already have a job. Besides, dirty as you are, a boy'd wear out his fingers scrubbing you clean."

The man laughed, then stumbled into the hotel and started singing.

Once he was out of sight, Vallie hooted. Wouldn't he just bust his buttons if he knew he'd asked a girl to wash his back?

I'd have bust my own buttons back in Allegheny if somebody had told me such a thing might happen, Vallie realized. *I'd have popped right out of my petticoats.* She bent over, laughing again at the thought. *Poor Aunt Margaret, I bet she never laughed this hard,* Vallie thought. *And the old me, back home, never did either. That old me couldn't have handled such a wild man, but the new me did just fine.* She swaggered down the street.

At the Silver Dollar, Nora was waiting with arms folded across her chest. "Thanks, Vallie. Those prospectors—when silver gets into the blood, there's no telling what a man might do."

But Papa's a prospector, Vallie thought with a start. *He'd never act like that. At least I hope not.*

By the time Peter Jensen arrived from his office a few minutes later, Vallie had scrubbed her hands and face and was setting the first full plates in front of a table of clean miners. Everyone was talking about the prospector and his rowdy spree.

"How long do you suppose it'll take for him to lose his silver?"

"He'll have trouble writing down the claim," another man said.

"Or remembering where it is," said the first man. "Give me a solid job any day. You work your shift, you earn your three dollars. You won't get rich, but you won't act the fool either."

The men were still discussing the prospector when Bo Reston's friend Bramblet Willis entered the Silver Dollar with a group of miners. He walked straight over to Vallie. "I heard there was a fracas here earlier. You all right? Bo's heading for Leadville again and asked me to keep an eye out for you while he's gone." The man had a serious look on his face, angry almost.

"I'm fine," Vallie said. "Fella was just loud and smelly. Want supper?"

Bramblet nodded. "I was bringing you something anyway. Might as well have a meal. What's Nora cooking?"

"Chicken and dumplings."

"Fine. This is for you." He passed her a package wrapped in brown paper and tied up with string. "Saw you coming out of the claims office earlier. If you find your pa's mine, you'll need these." He smiled.

She untied the string and slipped the paper open.

"It's a pair of Levi Strauss trousers. If you've a mind to go traipsing off looking for a mine, those flimsy city-boy duds won't be much use."

"Thanks."

"If they don't fit right, you can trade them at the mercantile. Now how about that supper?"

As Vallie made her way back to the kitchen, she took several deep breaths. Bramblet Willis was being very nice to her, but he hardly knew her. It didn't make much sense. Still, if Bo had asked him to keep a lookout . . .

She sorted out the possibilities. Maybe Bramblet was a softhearted man who took pity on strays the way she had with those kittens. But he'd looked angry at first. And he'd brought her a present. Why would a perfect stranger do such a thing? She frowned, uneasy. She'd handled the drunken prospector just fine, but Bramblet's interest was puzzling. Bothersome.

Spooked, Vallie told herself, *I'm just spooked by that crazy fellow. It can't hurt to be cautious, though. I'm not who I'm pretending to be, so I can't be a hundred percent sure of anybody else either.*

At the midnight shift change, Vallie still hadn't shaken off her uneasy feeling. She stepped outside briefly, in the minutes between the clean miners' suppers and the dirty ones', and looked toward Aspen Mountain. Again she saw a line of tiny lights curving up the mountain.

"What are those lights?" she asked Peter, who stood close by at the bar. "Like stars on the mountain?"

"Gad hunters," he replied. "Tin cans or lard buckets with holes punched through and a tallow candle.

You'll only see them at midnight, when the night shifts change. Miners use them to light their way up and down the mountain. Makes a pretty sight, doesn't it?"

"It sure does." Later, when Vallie lay stretched out on the cot, she heard soft mewing. She climbed out of bed and picked Josie up.

"Sorry. I've been so busy, I forgot about you," she whispered. "That's a bad idea, with Peter's deadline coming along on Friday." She smiled in the darkness. "By Friday, all our troubles will be over. I'll find Papa and then I can keep you and Patsy myself."

Josie meowed, a sweet small sound. "You like that idea too, don't you? I guess you know Papa's a soft touch when it comes to critters."

She tried to bring her father's face to mind, but instead, she saw the dirty prospector's wild grin, and unexpectedly, the serious face of Bramblet Willis. *What is that man really after?* she wondered.

18

The Annabelle

Vallie returned to the mining claims office after breakfast on Tuesday morning and began poring over the books. After meeting her first successful prospector, it no longer surprised her that the handwriting was hard to read. Still, her eyes stung and she had to take a few minutes every hour to rub them and look out on the mountains for a diversion.

Two-thirty came quickly, almost time to return to the café, but Vallie had only a few pages to read in the second ledger. Her eyes were so tired, she almost missed it, but the handwriting on the next to last page caught her attention. The Annabelle Mine. Mama's name. She scanned the page, barely breathing.

Discovery Notice

THE ANNABELLE MINING CLAIM · JULY 2, 1884

I claim by right of discovery and location 1,500 *feet*

along this lode located on Aspen Mountain due south of the mine known as the Dusty Jack. I claim 700 feet running northerly from the center of the location and 800 feet running southerly from the center of said claim with one hundred and fifty feet upon either side thereof.

DANIEL HARPER

Papa! Papa, I found you at last!

Vallie jumped up from the table and showed the ledger book to the bald man who worked in the claims office. "How would I find this mine, please? Is there a map?" Her voice trembled.

"Might be. Let me take a look at that book."

Vallie shifted her weight from side to side as the man read the notice. *Hurry up, hurry up. I have to find the Annabelle!* He frowned and stepped back toward a map that lined one wall, muttering to himself.

"The Dusty Jack, the Dusty Jack. Ah, here we go. There's the Dusty Jack. Just below Tourtelotte Park. Look here."

Vallie edged close to the map and examined where the man pointed. "If your pa's mine is south of the Dusty Jack, shouldn't be hard to find. Right up there on the big mountain."

"I could find it?"

"It'll take a while. An hour, maybe." He looked

down at her feet. "You got good boots, boy. If your legs are sturdy, you should make it easy enough."

"Yes, sir. I walked seventy miles through Independence Pass, I guess I can climb one mountain." She turned toward the door. "Thank you, sir."

"Now hold up, boy. Let's sketch you a map so you get to the right part of the mountain. No point traipsing off to the wrong mine."

He sketched quickly, then passed her the paper. "Good luck, lad."

She dashed out the door and headed right for the mountain. She'd be letting Nora and Peter down when she missed her shift, but with Papa so close, she didn't need to work in the Silver Dollar anymore. *At least tell them where you're off to,* her conscience scolded, but she ignored the nagging voice. If she told, they'd keep her from searching until after work.

Vallie began her climb at the end of Galena Street as the sketch suggested. The first slope of the mountain wasn't too steep, but soon the pitch increased. Her breathing grew strained and she had to slow down, but every minute she wasted was a minute she couldn't see Papa, so she pushed as fast as she could.

The lower part of the mountain had been partly cleared of trees, and Vallie found a rough path that seemed to point in the right direction. And sure enough, as she climbed and sweated her way up, she heard voices and the clank of machines. Papa's mine!

The sounds grew louder, and soon she could see a clearing with buildings and machines and mules. She hurried on, ignoring the sting in her lungs. Finally she reached the first shed. A man stood inside the doorway covered in grime, his eyes white against the sooty skin of his face. The old Vallie would have been scared by such a man, but the new one wasn't; she'd served plenty of meals to dirty miners.

She tried to catch her breath. "Excuse me, sir, but is this the Annabelle Mine? Or the Dusty Jack?"

The man shook his head at her. "This here's the Unity Mine."

She fumbled for the rough map and showed it to him.

"I don't know nothing about no Annabelle nor Dusty Jack. You'd best talk to the boss. He's up in the main shed." The man pointed.

"Thanks for the help." Vallie hurried on. *I must have made a little mistake in direction,* she thought, *but surely I'm close.*

When she reached the largest shed, the machines clanked and echoed. Two men stood in a corner, watching a large wheel turn. The thundering metal machines made her feel tiny. "Excuse me," she shouted. "I'm looking for the Annabelle Mine. Can you help me?"

One of the men nodded and walked toward the door. Outside, he walked several feet from the shed where the noise wasn't quite so ferocious. "What was that?" he asked.

"I'm looking for my father's mine. The Annabelle. It's supposed to be here, south of the Dusty Jack. Am I in the wrong place?"

"Right place, wrong name," the man said. "This is the Unity Mine. We've been working here since late last summer. Used to be called Dusty Jack, Annabelle, and three or four others."

"I don't understand," Vallie began.

"Investors bought up a whole passel of small claims. Spent a pretty penny they did too."

"And the Annabelle was one? You're sure?" Vallie's throat tightened.

"Sure as Sunday." He studied her face. "Now, don't look so glum. If your pa had a claim up here, he's made himself a pile of money. He's probably out finding a new mine right this minute. A person gets good luck once, it sticks to him."

Vallie took a deep breath. "Thanks. Thanks a lot." She turned and hurried downhill before he could see the tears pooling up in her eyes. *Good luck isn't the only thing that sticks to a person,* she thought. *Bad luck's been sticking to me for a long time.*

In the hour it took to climb down the mountain, Vallie had plenty of time to worry about being late. Nora was strict, and she had that sign about how to behave. She'd probably add another line to the sign now—NO SKIPPING WORK TO LOOK FOR FATHERS. When she arrived at the Silver Dollar, Nora stood with her hands on her hips and glared. "Where have you been?"

"Up on the mountain. I thought I'd found Papa's mine. And I did. But it isn't his anymore. I'm sorry, I—"

"You're a sorry sight, is what. I had to serve two sets of suppers and cook everything."

"I'm sorry, Nora. I made a mistake."

"Maybe I made the mistake, hiring you."

Nora was right, but Vallie wished the woman would stop hollering and try to understand.

"No, you didn't. I'm a good worker. I won't let you down again."

"Shouldn't have let me down the first time. If I thought I could find another boy . . ."

"Please. I won't run off. I promise, I'll save my searching for when you don't need me."

"Well, I need you now and that's a fact. Boys looking for work are scarce in this town. Have a go at that pile of dirty dishes." Nora strode out of the kitchen.

At least I haven't lost my job, Vallie thought, turning toward the sink. Plates jumbled everywhere, and in the café, more tables waited to be cleared. She pumped water and set it on the stove to warm. Then she began the endless chore of scraping and stacking. *I really shouldn't complain. I still have food to eat and a place to stay.*

But with every plate, her fingers gripped the dishcloth harder. She scrubbed away grease as if it were dirt from Papa's mine, the mine he hadn't cared enough about to keep. "You called it the Annabelle after Mama," she argued to the mountain of dirty dishes. "And then you went and sold it. What kind of person does a thing like that, Papa? You were never hard-hearted before."

She slumped over the sink and attacked the silverware next, trying to ignore a new worry that buzzed in her mind. But like a pesky fly, once the idea came, she couldn't get rid of it. She poked the palm of her hand with a fork, hoping the pain would silence the notion, but that only made the voice in her mind whisper louder.

You've changed a lot, Valentine, in just a couple of weeks since leaving Pennsylvania. Your papa's been gone for more than a year, so without a doubt he's changed too. Wake up, girl, face facts.

She closed her eyes tight, not wanting to imagine who she might find when she finally located that man named Daniel Harper.

19

The Valentine

Peter Jensen spoke to Vallie as she scowled her way through the late shift that night. "Nora says you found a mine your pa discovered."

"Fat lot of good it did. My father sold his mine."

"And I suppose my Nora scorched your ears for being late."

"Yes, sir, she did. I . . . I guess I deserve it."

"That Nora . . . She's a good woman, but firm-minded. Not much softness left these days. Not that I blame her."

"I'm sorry, sir. It's just that I thought I'd found Papa. And I hadn't."

"But you found his claim. It's a good sign. If he found one mine, it's likely he's found another. I'd keep looking in those books if I were you."

Vallie shrugged. "I guess. Can't think of anything else to try."

And so with every spare minute on Wednesday, she read mining claims from the previous July and August. At the end of the day she had nothing to show for it but stinging eyes. On her way back to the Silver Dollar, she stopped at the post office, just on the chance that something might have arrived for Papa.

"Sorry," the postmaster said. "Nothing for Daniel Harper. But are you Valentine?"

"Yes. Why?"

"Letter for you, then." He flipped through a stack of envelopes and passed her one. "Good day now."

Vallie rushed outside. How could she be getting a letter? Nobody knew she was here. Her fingers shook as she ripped open the envelope and saw Bridget's familiar handwriting.

Valentine My Girl,

If you are reading this, then I've guessed right and you're in Colorado with your father. Can't say I approve of your methods, but I don't blame you much either. In case you were wondering, the house here is in a tizzy. The missus worries and pesters the mister. He storms around and blusters. Your cousin tries to make himself scarce.

A warning to you. Your uncle has set detectives after you, Pinkertons, they're called. He's busy at the telegraph office every morning. So do watch out. But if you're with your father, surely they can't be sticking their long noses into your business, can they?

I myself have kept my mouth shut, or nearly so. I found an odd and suspicious note to your teacher, which I burned in the stove. When the mister interviewed me and asked if I had a notion of where you'd gone or why, I did mention that his son had been pulling mischief, and that most girls would take offense at dead mice in their beds and favorite dolls torn to pieces. He narrowed those cold blue eyes of his, but he didn't tell me I was wrong either. So young Harold is none too cozy these days. With you a safe distance away, and I hope you are, I thought I'd let a bit of the truth slip out.

I suppose you felt you couldn't say goodbye, and you're right. I might have tried to stop you. Unless I'd have decided to ride along myself! Wouldn't that have been grand, now? I've examined my conscience and decided that I'm not obliged to tell your uncle my suspicions, for I'm employed by your father after all, and doesn't he want what's best for his Valentine?

But I do wonder, how was it you made the trip? And what will you and your dear father be doing next? And does it require the assistance of your friend,

Bridget Joyce

Vallie read the letter a second time with teary eyes. Dear, lovely Bridget had taken her side and even told on Harold. She should have known she could trust her friend.

Rereading the letter brought Bridget's pale freckled

face to mind. "The minute I find Papa," Vallie promised. "I'll write you a good long letter, Bridget, and apologize for everything. I just hope it's soon."

It took until late afternoon on Friday to find another mention of Papa in the claims office. Vallie's breath caught at the entry. The Valentine Mine. He'd named it for her!

Oh, Papa. I've found you for sure this time. Her father had claimed an area up on a place called Shadow Mountain late last fall.

When she showed it to the bald man behind the desk, he smiled. "Made the claim just as the first snows were flying," he said. "Probably had to hurry to get the land staked and marked before really bad weather hit."

"Where's Shadow Mountain? Can you show me on a map?"

The man nodded. "If you stand at the foot of Aspen Mountain and look to the west, you'll see a dip at the summit, then another rise. That's Shadow Mountain, right up there on the shoulder of the main mountain. Casts a long afternoon shadow on the town, it does. There's been less mining up there, so my maps aren't complete." He studied the claim notice, then pointed to his big map. "From what he wrote, his claim is situated on the side facing town. You'd want to start climbing about here, on Durant Avenue, and look for a chalky ledge, about halfway up. Could take an hour or so to reach the mine."

Vallie tried to memorize everything he said.

"The last time I went up to a mine it had been sold. Will that happen this time too?"

"Can't say." He frowned and thought for a moment. "But it isn't likely. He's still got to patent the claim, and drag a buyer out to study it—nobody's going to buy a mine sight unseen. Besides which, from October till April, the mountains have been covered with snow. Men have just started venturing out and about again since the mud's dried up. I'd say you have a good chance of finding your pa's claim this time."

Papa's claim, not Papa. "Thanks." Vallie hurried back to the Silver Dollar. This time she knew better than to run off without telling anyone. Sure enough, Nora expected her to work her regular hours, but Peter offered to walk a ways with her the next day.

When the café opened for supper, Bramblet Willis came in and took a corner table. "Roast beef, and an extra ladle of Nora's brown gravy," he said with a smile. "Piping hot."

"Sure thing," Vallie said. She straightened the silverware at his place.

"You're looking mighty perky tonight," he said. "Good news?"

"Yes, sir. The best news. I found the claim for Papa's mine today. Up on Shadow Mountain. And guess what? He named his mine for me!"

"Congratulations. That *is* good news." He smiled.

"I'll go find it tomorrow and wear those Levi trousers you gave me. I've been saving them."

"Best of luck, then."

Vallie hurried into the kitchen with his order. Nora served it up and poured a second ladleful of gravy over the beef and mashed potatoes.

"Carry it careful now," she warned. "Plate's full and hot."

"Yes, ma'am."

Vallie walked slowly from the kitchen into the main room of the café. The heat from the plate stung her fingers. As she neared Bramblet's table, she noticed that another man had joined him, sitting in the shadows.

She took two steps closer before a quick motion from the strange man froze her in place. He pulled a long, cruel-looking hunting knife from under the table and pointed it right at Bramblet's chest. "Found you at last, Willis, you dirty swine," the man said. "Now you'll pay."

Without stopping to think, Vallie rushed to the table and dumped the steaming plate onto the man's lap. He yelled and jumped back.

His knife fell to the floor.

Men jumped up and within seconds, Peter and several dirty miners had dragged the man outside.

"Lousy scum! Stinking Pinkerton!" the man yelled.

The words rang in Vallie's ears. *Pinkerton? Bramblet Willis?*

Nora rushed in from the kitchen. "What's all that commotion? Vallie, what have you done to yourself?"

Vallie looked down. Gravy and mashed potatoes dripped from her shirt and trousers. "A man. With a knife. Pointing it at Bramblet. He's . . ."

"Go on, get changed. I'll bring you water and a fresh towel." Nora shooed Vallie toward the kitchen and hurried outside, where men's loud voices could still be heard.

Vallie stumbled into the kitchen. Now that it was all over, her hands shook and she felt icy cold. A Pinkerton. Bramblet Willis was a Pinkerton detective. If he hadn't already figured out who she was, it wouldn't take him long. She had to get herself out of town right away.

In her room she pulled off her boots and trousers, then unbuttoned her food-covered shirt and dropped it to the floor.

"Vallie? Are you all right, boy? Not burned, are you?"

Nora! Vallie spun around, snatching up her clean shirt and covering her chest with it.

Nora stood, gaping, in the open doorway with a towel and a pail of water. "Vallie? Put that shirt down."

"No, ma'am. I can't." Vallie didn't have full, womanly curves yet, but she didn't look like a little boy anymore either.

Nora scowled. "Valentine?" She stepped closer and yanked on the shirt. "A girl?"

Vallie grabbed her shirt, turned her back to Nora and fumbled with the buttons. She pulled on the Levi trousers and stuck her feet into her boots. When she turned around, Nora still stood there, frozen like a statue.

"I can't believe you fooled us all."

From the crate under the cot, a kitten mewed.

"You kept those darn cats too. They're supposed to be gone by now."

"I'm sorry. I was hoping tomorrow . . . for the kittens . . . I . . ."

"Tomorrow, then. You and the cats will both be gone by first light. We don't cotton to liars here. You understand?"

"I'll leave right away. Tonight. I'm sorry. It was wrong, but I had good reasons. . . ."

"No good reasons for lying. Not ever."

Nora slammed the door, and Vallie sank to the cot. She reached underneath and pulled out the crate, lifting out both kittens and burying her nose in their soft fur. "Now what?" she sniffed. "Where do we go from here?"

There was only one place Vallie could think of. Papa's mine. She finished dressing, flung her belongings into her satchel, stuck a kitten into each jacket pocket and charged out of the room.

A scowling Nora guarded the back door as if she were the detective. She thrust coins into Vallie's hand, and a basket. "Here's what you're owed, and a day's food. Nobody can say I didn't treat you square. Now git."

Vallie bolted from the door and raced along the dark, dusty streets. Her boots echoed and her satchel weighed heavy on her shoulder. In each jacket pocket a kitten curled, ready for sleep.

But Vallie couldn't sleep. She had to escape from that Pinkerton and find the Valentine. And now she had to do it in the dark.

20

On Shadow Mountain

There wasn't much of a moon. Vallie needed a gad hunter like the miners used to find her way up the dark face of Shadow Mountain, but she didn't have one. She stumbled against rocks and slipped on loose gravel. A mountain breeze poked cold fingers down the collar of her jacket and she shivered.

It could take an hour or so in the daytime to reach the place where the rock face flattened out, the man had said. At night it could take forever. In the darkness, she could only see a few feet ahead, so she watched her footing carefully, avoided the shadowy trees and prayed she didn't get lost.

One foot after another, she trudged upward, skirting patches of slippery gravel. As she climbed on, her eyes began to pick out shapes. The shadows grew less murky and finally she could see the ledge above her.

Legs burning, she made her way around a huge boulder and then another, looking for a place where she could climb onto the ledge. On her right, a tumble of broken stone made climbing impossible. Vallie turned to the left and looked uphill, where she saw a distant, rectangular shadow that didn't look like the rest of the mountain.

Her heart thundered, and she scrambled on until she stood right in front of a wooden shack. Papa's or not, she and the kittens could stay the night here unless somebody else had claimed it. Did she dare knock?

Vallie trembled and she had to catch her breath as she reached out with one hand to touch the door, fastened shut with a string. "Hello. Anyone here?"

No answer. She tugged the door open and stepped inside. Without windows, the shack was even darker than the night and so shadowy she could barely make out shapes. A rough cot. A barrel. And it was empty.

She dropped her satchel on the barrel, lifted the kittens out of her pockets and set them on the dirt floor. "We're here, girls. It's not much, but it has a roof and a door. Run around, now. I'll get food."

The kittens tumbled into every corner. They poked their heads out the door and returned, sniffing and rubbing against Vallie's ankles. The packet of food contained a healthy supply of cold roast beef and bread. Vallie tore off small strips of the meat and set them on the floor for the kittens before she plopped down on the cot to eat her own share.

As she finished eating, Vallie felt waves of fatigue wash over her. At her feet, the kittens batted the laces of her boots. She lifted them gently onto the cot. "Bedtime, girls. We've had quite a night. And a busy day tomorrow, unless I miss my guess."

Vallie made sure the door was shut, returned to the cot, leaned back and closed her eyes. From somewhere nearby she heard howling. She'd heard those sounds at night from the safety of her room at the Silver Dollar and always thought they were dogs. Here on Shadow Mountain she was close enough to realize they were coyotes. Shivering, she gathered the kittens closer. She'd heard folks complain in town that the critters hunted at night and made off with people's pets. "I bet they can smell us," she whispered to Josie and Patsy. "And the roast beef too. Stay close to me, girls."

What am I thinking? Vallie asked herself. *Am I really expecting these babies to comfort me? That's not how it works. I've got it backward.*

She sat up again and leaned against the rough wooden wall of the cabin, cradling the tiny, warm bodies in her lap. It would be a long, cold night, and somebody bigger than a coyote needed to keep watch. Vallie forced her eyes to stay open. As the night wore on, the howling grew more distant and she let herself curl on the cot with the kittens and doze.

The clatter of hoofbeats against rock woke Vallie and she bolted upright. "What? Who?" Around her, pale threads of morning light showed between the rough boards of the shack's walls. The events of the night before rushed back and she covered her face with her hands.

"Oh, kitties, someone's coming. Maybe it's Papa."

Vallie stumbled to her feet and pushed open the door a crack, watching the mountainside as the hoofbeats grew louder and slowed. Downhill and to her left, a shape emerged from the aspen trees. A man, wearing a cowboy hat and riding a horse.

As the rider neared she recognized pale hair and a thick beard—Bramblet Willis, coming to send her back. Disappointment washed over her like cold creek water. And fear. She couldn't go back to Pennsylvania, not when she'd come so far. All her instincts told her to run, but she stayed put. A girl on foot couldn't outrun a man on a horse.

Bramblet neared the large boulders below, reined up, climbed off his horse and carefully walked the last of the distance to the shack.

In her mind, Vallie readied her arguments against being sent home. She'd found both of Papa's mines in that claims book, so she'd find Papa himself soon. He'd return any day to protect his property. She just needed time.

"Valentine." Bramblet's voice came so softly, Vallie wasn't sure she'd heard him. She eased the door open and the kittens raced out.

Bramblet stepped closer and hitched his horse to a sapling. "I'm sorry about last night. I'd hoped to tell you who I was myself, but that fella at the café upset the apple cart. Could I sit down, please?" He took off his hat.

Vallie stepped outside. She avoided looking into his eyes, studying his dusty boots instead. "Sure."

He dropped to a flat rock. "So you found your pa's mine." He pointed to a sign over the shack's door. THE VALENTINE. "Good for you."

Vallie hadn't noticed the sign when she'd arrived in the dark. So this was Papa's claim after all. Finding it should have been a moment of triumph, but her heart felt dry and sore instead.

She sat in the doorway, lifted her eyes and met Bramblet's. "Why is it good? So I can see the mine before you haul me back to my uncle?" She spat the words at him.

"Vallie, please . . ." His eyes gleamed green in the sun.

"What? You're a Pinkerton. You're working for Uncle Franklin, aren't you?"

He brushed his fingers along the brim of his hat. "Yes, I am. But what makes you think I aim to haul you back?"

"You found me." She scowled.

"I found you a few days ago, Vallie. I haven't hauled you anyplace yet."

"Why not?"

"First off, this is the end of the line. You couldn't leave town without me hearing about it. Besides, until that sidewinder showed up with a knife, I'd kept my Pinkerton activities quiet. Pretty hard to be a detective in disguise if everybody and his aunt Maude sees me haul you down Cooper Avenue."

That stopped her. "What about my uncle? You told him where I landed, didn't you?" The kittens clambered into her lap and settled into soft balls of orange fluff.

"I've wired him and he's wired back, a number of times."

"I don't understand. Uncle Franklin doesn't want you to send me back? Oh wait, I get it. He's glad to be rid of me. He had you look for me, just to make sure I wasn't dead or something, but now . . ." She sniffed and couldn't continue. She rubbed at her eyes.

He set the hat aside. "Valentine, you're getting ahead of yourself. Could I just explain what's happened?"

She looked at him sideways. "I guess. But tell the truth. Bo Reston said you were his friend. A rancher."

"I am his friend. We grew up on neighboring farms in Mississippi. Came out West after soldiering together." He let out a big sigh. "I'm a rancher, nowadays. I used to work full time for the Pinkertons in Denver, but when news came of a silver strike in a beautiful mountain valley, Bo and me, we came here to take a look and both decided to settle. I spend most of my time down the river a ways, running cattle and breeding mules and horses. Bo buys his mules from me and hauls goods back and forth across the pass."

As he spoke, Vallie watched his face closely. He didn't look like a man spinning a fable. She was inclined to believe him, if not forgive him. "You're still a detective. You were after me."

"Yes. I do a job now and again. The Pinkertons wired me a couple weeks back to be on the lookout for a runaway girl, so I watched the post office and the stagecoach depot for a few days. That reminds me—just a minute."

He stood and stepped to his horse. He reached for something Vallie couldn't quite see; then he turned. "I believe this belongs to you." He passed her a large wooden box, *her box,* with the twine still tied around it.

The box felt heavy and familiar in her lap. Vallie

twisted the ends of the twine. Her voice stuck in her throat. "Um . . ." She swallowed.

"When this and your ticket showed up in the Denver depot without you, it kicked up quite a ruckus. Pinkertons held on to it for a day or two, hoping you'd claim it. If that had happened, the detective in Denver would have probably bought a pair of tickets and ridden back East with you."

Vallie set the box down gently in the dirt. "Well, I didn't claim it. I figured Uncle Franklin would be searching for me. So I left it."

"Smart. When you didn't show in Denver, they wired me to watch for you here, and I did. Then after a day or so, your uncle decided you must have met with an accident on your way out from Chicago."

Vallie frowned. "An accident? Why?"

Bramblet shrugged. "They found a box and a ticket, but no Valentine Harper. You were just a young girl, unprotected. What else would he think? Anyway, your uncle instructed the Pinkerton Agency to search hospitals and undertakers from Chicago to Denver. They told me to stop wasting my time."

Vallie shook her head, disgusted. "You found me anyway."

"That was luck. Bo hauled a load of grain down to my ranch for my animals. Told me about this tough young boy who'd wrestled his way across the pass with the jack train in search of his father.

The story made my ears perk up, so I asked your name."

"And it matched." Vallie scuffed at the dirt. "So you told Bo and my uncle about me and now everyone knows and you're going to send me back."

"Hold on, Valentine. I told Bo I'd heard of a youngster who'd run off and might be looking for his pa. Didn't say you were a girl. Figured that was your business."

"All right. What about telling Uncle Franklin?"

"Bo talked me into waiting. Said you had grit and determination and ought to get a chance of finding your pa on your own. So I watched you awhile before I wired your uncle. Then, when I did send the message, I asked him to give you a little more time."

"Why?"

"Bo was right. You had a job and a place to stay by the time I met you. The Jensens are good people; you weren't in any danger that I could see. Besides which, you'd hauled yourself halfway across the country with no help. Figured you were spunky enough, you might find your pa. Then I'd be out of a job."

"And my uncle agreed?"

"Yep. He wasn't real specific, but he said as long as you weren't in any danger, he'd give me a few days."

"He just wants to be rid of me."

"You're jumping to conclusions, girl. I don't remember the words your uncle used, but I got the feeling he thought *you* might be better off *here,* if you could find your pa."

"If," Vallie said. She bit down hard on her bottom lip. *If* was an awfully big word for only two letters.

21

A Girl Again

"You want to tell me why you ran off? And how you managed? Lots of grown women couldn't have done it alone, you know. You're a plucky girl."

So Vallie spilled her story, with lots of questions from Bramblet, until she felt tired and empty. All she seemed to be able to do was pet the kittens.

"What will you do with me now that I lost my job?" she asked. "Since everybody knows I'm a girl."

He ran his hand through his whiskers again. "Well, if this were a usual case, I'd head for town, get us seats on the next stage and take you home. But it isn't a usual case."

"Why not?" Vallie didn't want to get her hopes up, but it seemed as if Bramblet might let her stay and keep looking for Papa.

"First off, I promised Bo I'd keep an eye on you,

not send you back East. Besides, I admire your spunk. The West is full of people with grit, people who aren't afraid to start off for a new place. I did it myself years ago after the war—left my troubles and my old life behind. I'd have fought tooth and nail if somebody'd tried to haul me back to Mississippi."

"So you'll let me stay?"

"If you can find your pa. I'd never forgive myself if I sent you back and he arrived the day after you left and you missed each other. Besides, I owe you, for last night. I might have an ugly cut, or worse, without your quick thinking."

"What will you do, then?"

"I don't know. You could stay with the housekeeper at my ranch and I could go look for your pa."

"But *I* found his mine."

"Yep. You're a pretty good detective yourself." He looked around, from the shack to the bare rock ledge below. "Now that you found it, though, I hope you're not planning to stay up here on the mountain waiting for your pa. It's an hour from town and you're a young girl alone. . . ."

"I won't stay long. If you aren't going to haul me back, I might go into town this afternoon and look for another job. A girl job this time."

"You don't have to do that. I owe you, Valentine. Least I can do is feed you and give you a place to stay."

It sounded tempting, but Vallie shook her head.

"Thanks, but I want to be in town, close to the mine. I can't find Papa downriver at your ranch."

"Makes sense. But if you can't find a job, you come see me." He pulled a pencil and a scrap of paper from his shirt pocket and began scribbling. "Give this to John Russell at the livery stable behind the post office. He'll cart you out to my ranch if you want."

"Thanks." She stuck the paper in her pocket. "How long do I have? Before you send me back to my uncle?"

"How's a week sound? Your uncle's a reasonable man, but he does worry about you."

"Just a week? That's not enough time."

"Come on, Vallie. Don't go soft on me now. You found his mine, didn't you?"

"Yes. Two of them. Lucky for me he hasn't sold this one."

"Wait a minute." Bramblet slapped his leg. "There's one place you haven't tried yet. If he sold his first mine—we've got a chance."

"What?"

"Here's my notion. A man sells a mine, and gets a big chunk of cash, he needs a safe place to keep it."

"You mean a bank? My uncle works in a bank."

"*The* bank. There's only one out here, the Jerome B. Wheeler Bank. Now, asking questions in a bank is a job for a Pinkerton. Do I have your permission to speak to the manager?"

"But what could the bank tell you?"

"We don't know until we ask. Do I have your permission?"

"Sure. Go ahead." A tiny flicker of hope kindled inside Vallie, small and faraway-feeling, like one of those gad hunters on the mountain. But she was afraid to trust it; she'd hoped before and been disappointed.

Bramblet stood and offered Vallie a hand to pull her to her feet. "For now, I'll just say goodbye and good luck, then." He shook her hand, then put his hat back on his head and walked toward his horse.

She watched him leave. He seemed a nice man, that Bramblet Willis, Pinkerton or not.

Vallie sat in the doorway of the shack as the morning sun rose higher. Once the sound of Bramblet's horse had disappeared, she lifted her wooden box and picked at the knots. Her fingers trembled and she had to slow down.

At last she untangled the twine and slipped the lid off. Inside the box, everything was just as she'd last seen it. Her shawl on top, packed tightly around Maria and the photographs of Mama and Papa. Clothing underneath, her own clothes. As she touched the smooth cotton of her yellow gingham dress, her eyes filled. She could be a girl again!

"First things first," she told the kittens. "A proper girl would never be as dirty as I am. I need a bath. And you two need some food."

She gathered the kittens and set out some roast beef for them inside the shack. "What do I need, girls, what do I need?" A wooden shelf along one wall held a tin bucket, and Vallie lifted it down. "Let's see, a dress, petticoats, and a set of clean underwear. Do I remember how to dress like a girl? It's been a while. Be good while I'm gone, kitties."

Vallie grabbed a hunk of bread and stepped outside. Latching the door securely, she set off downhill, munching and looking for water. Last night had been too dark for her to see much, but if she didn't find a stream nearby and had to return to town she could do it; it was only an hour's walk. Three rivers ran near the town—surely she could find a private place to bathe in one of them.

The slopes of Shadow Mountain didn't feel nearly so steep by daylight. Down below, the town spread out, filling the narrow valley. Above and to her right, distant smoke and noise marked the sites of working mines. Nearing a patch of trees, she heard a soft ripple of water over stones and followed the sound.

It wasn't much, as creeks went, but a thin stream of

water splashed down between the rocks and she could fill her bucket. She looked around. Not a soul in sight unless you counted the pair of gray jaybirds that scolded from an aspen branch overhead. Setting her girl clothes in a patch of grass, she wedged the bucket under the spill of water.

She skinned off her boots, Harold's trousers and shirt, her underwear and socks. Taking a deep breath, she poured the bucketful over her head. "Ouch! That stings," she complained to the jays. "Why didn't you warn me about the ice water? Or maybe you did and I misunderstood."

The jays kept up their squawking, and Vallie was glad of their company. Gooseflesh pebbled her body all over. She set the bucket down to fill again and scrubbed at her skin and short hair. She poured a second pail over herself, shivering and grumbling aloud. "This water's as cold as the snow in Independence Pass. Bet it comes from melting snow!"

She collected a third pail for a final rinse then dried herself with the shirt she'd been wearing and fluffed her hair. Stepping into her lacy spring underwear, Vallie had the sensation of moving backward in time. In her mind, she returned to her room at Aunt Margaret's house. The cloth felt so crisp against her skin, so clean—the starch in the petticoats, the ironing, even the stitching were a comfort. She lifted her own dress over her head and felt rich, a millionaire, as if she'd been the one to discover a silver mine.

The jays jabbered. *Good for you,* Vallie imagined the birds had said.

Back at the shack, the kittens nosed into her box as she unpacked. She laid Maria on the cot and set Mama and Papa's photographs on the barrel. "Even a rough shed can look homey, right, girls?"

As she arranged her belongings, the layers of petticoats tangled about her legs. Patsy and Josie batted at the ruffles and boot laces, which made it even harder for Vallie to walk. "This is foolish! Wearing such big boots with skirts would tangle anybody. I'll change and go pick us some flowers."

She sat and removed the boots and socks, slipping her feet into a pair of soft kid slippers. Outside, she made her way to a patch of bright yellow flowers, but still her petticoats tangled and dust collected on her slippers. When she stepped into a patch of loose gravel, her left foot slipped and she went down with a thump.

Fancy shoes were meant for town, not for the mountains, she realized, brushing the dust off her skirts. So were all those petticoats. Bending, she filled her milk bottle with water and arranged the yellow flowers. Then she sat and peeled off two of the petticoats, and traded her fancy shoes for the sturdy boots. Better. Much more comfortable.

Vallie touched her hair. The curls had dried, and she poked one of the yellow flowers behind her right ear. She was dressed like a girl again at long last, but with short, chopped-off hair and thick boots on, what sort of drab girl did she look like?

22

Toby

I'm not the sort of girl who's going to mope about short hair or not enough petticoats, Vallie decided. She had only a week to find Papa and she was wasting time. The sun had climbed high in the sky, so it must be nearly noon. If she planned to look for a job, she might as well get started.

Hitching up her skirts, Vallie marched down the mountain. She went straight to the newspaper office to read the classified advertisements, but an article on the front page of *The Aspen Times* stopped her.

SILVER DOLLAR BOY SAVES LOCAL RANCHER
HERO SCALDS ASSAILANT, THEN DISAPPEARS

On Friday afternoon, as many were sitting to eat their suppers, a stranger took a seat at the Silver Dollar Café, but not to dine. The man, Hiram Mosely, had a darker purpose. He'd tracked his quarry to Aspen and followed him into the café with evil intent and a sharp knife. After pulling said knife on Mr. Charles "Bramblet" Willis, who runs the C-W Ranch northwest of Aspen, Mr. Mosely got the surprise of his life. Valentine Harper, who lately works at the café, poured a plate of hot gravy into Mosely's lap, causing him to drop the knife. Mr. Willis, café owner Peter Jensen and several miners escorted a disarmed Mosely to the sheriff's office, where all were questioned and the culprit dispatched to jail.

When interrogated, Hiram Mosely admitted a motive of revenge. It seems that three years ago, in the spring of 1882, Mr. Mosely was caught in possession of a large shipment of goods which belonged to his previous employer, Brown's Mercantile, in Denver. His theft was uncovered by the excellent detective work of Mr. Willis, a sometimes employee of the Pinkerton Detective Agency.

Mr. Willis and Mr. Jensen both commended the bravery and quick thinking of Valentine Harper. However, when this reporter searched out the lad, he'd disappeared from sight. Should he reappear, it would be gratifying to hear his side of this very exciting tale.

Vallie scanned the article again. *Guess Nora didn't tell him I was a girl.* Except the part about her being a lad, the reporter had told it exactly as it had happened. *Oh boy,* she thought, *wait till I can send this to*

Bridget. And I'll show it to Papa, when I find him. They called me a hero right on the front page. But I'll be a hungry hero if I don't find a job.

She turned to the advertisements and folded back the page. Most of the notices wanted men or boys. Only three seemed as if they might be willing to hire Vallie—two at rooming houses and one watching a child.

The rooming houses were both on Hopkins Avenue, only a block from the newspaper office, so she tried those first. In one house, the woman had already employed a miner's daughter to help with chores. In the other, the owner took a long look at Vallie and shook her head. "Young as you are, I doubt you know the first thing about tidying rooms. Sorry."

Vallie kept walking, crossing over Main Street toward Bleeker, to try for the last job. If this one didn't work out, she'd have to swallow her pride and go stay with Bramblet Willis after all. As she neared the address, she recognized the house. She'd offered kittens here to the small boy with the dogcart. Fortunately, she'd left the kittens back at Papa's shack today. And now she was dressed as a girl, in her yellow gingham dress, so perhaps they wouldn't remember.

She stepped around to the back door and knocked.

"One moment, please." A soft voice answered, sounding kind and polite. The door opened and a small, round, dark-haired woman smiled. "Yes?"

Vallie cleared her throat. "I've come about the job, ma'am. In the paper. It said you needed help."

"I do indeed. Come in." She stuck out her hand to shake Vallie's. "I'm Ivy Richardson."

"Valentine Harper." Vallie smiled and breathed in the smell of bread baking.

"Have you a strong constitution, Valentine?"

"I . . . I think so."

"It isn't an easy job, caring for Toby." The woman rubbed at her back. "He's something of an adventurer. Broke his leg, you see. And I'm not supposed to lift him just now. Doctor's orders." She placed one hand on her very rounded belly.

Vallie felt her cheeks warm. She looked away from the belly. "I've had an adventure or two myself," she began. "I'm not afraid of work."

"Come and meet Toby, then." The woman led her through the kitchen into a front parlor, where a little boy with reddish hair sat drawing. His right leg, propped on a pillow, still wore its splint. On the floor, the large black dog that had pulled the cart looked up at Vallie, then resumed his nap.

"Mama, look. I've drawn my jack. See, I got the ears right this time." He pointed to his paper.

Mrs. Richardson smiled. "*Your* jack indeed. Toby, I've brought you a friend. This is Valentine."

Toby looked up. "Why are you a girl now? Where are your kittens?"

His mother frowned. "Pardon me? Have you two met?"

Vallie's cheeks heated up again. "I can explain, ma'am. But you may not want to hire me. I was working at the Silver Dollar. And they had a litter of kittens. . . ."

"The Silver Dollar?" Toby asked. "Papa read at breakfast how a boy saved somebody from a man with a knife. Were you the Silver Dollar boy? Were you?"

Vallie closed her eyes.

"Valentine Harper. I knew that name sounded familiar." Mrs. Richardson seemed more curious than angry. "I read today's newspaper too. So which are you really, a boy or a girl?"

"I'm a girl, ma'am. It's a long story."

"She's the Silver Dollar Girl, then," Toby announced. "Hooray! I like stories. Don't leave any parts out."

"Yes, this does sound interesting," his mother added. "Please, sit down and tell us everything."

Vallie did as she was asked. She included the parts about Joseph and Patrick so that Mrs. Richardson would understand that she liked children.

"Can she be my nanny, Mama? Please?" Toby grinned at Vallie.

"Well, Valentine, you've behaved in an unconventional manner. But it sounds as if you'd be able to keep up with Toby," Mrs. Richardson said.

"Yes, ma'am."

The woman looked relieved. "He broke his leg climbing to the top of the fence, you know—"

"I was being a tightrope walker for the circus, Mama," he interrupted.

"Now you're a chariot driver," Vallie said. She reached down to scratch the floppy ears of the dog, who slept at her feet. "And this is your brave steed."

The mother smiled. "Shall we give it a try? Mr. Richardson will have to approve, of course, and he is a bit starchy. But even he's admitted that a frail, ruffled girl might find our Toby a handful."

"Yes, ma'am."

"If my husband approves, he'll discuss the arrangements. We have an attic room if you need a place to stay."

"Yes, please."

"Well, then. Perhaps you'll help Toby into his cart and harness up Thunder. The doctor has ordered fresh air and lots of sunshine."

"Could we walk by the rooming houses? I need to search for my father."

"Don't see why not. Toby, will you help Valentine find everything she needs?"

"Yes, Mama. Come on, Valentine. The cart's on the back porch. Let's hurry. I want to show you my jacks."

"Mules?" Vallie frowned.

"Yep. But you're good with mules—you came down the pass on a jack train, didn't you, Valentine?"

Vallie sighed. "Yes, Toby. I did." Mules again. Well, there were worse things, Vallie knew, like drunken prospectors and men with knives and coyotes in the night. She bent to help him from the chair. "Let's get you to your chariot. And call me Vallie. My friends do."

"Can I be your friend? Even if I'm only six and I've got a busted leg?"

"Sure. I'd say we could both use a friend."

Toby didn't weigh much, and he was helpful, showing her how to strap Thunder into the harness. "Snitch some sugar lumps from the kitchen, Vallie," he instructed her. "And a carrot. We've got to go visit my jacks."

"But your mother . . ."

"Thunder's tired of playing horse," Toby said.

Vallie stepped into the kitchen. Mrs. Richardson was tapping a fresh, fragrant loaf of bread from its pan.

"Um. Might I have a carrot, please?" Vallie began. "And Toby said I should snitch some sugar."

Mrs. Richardson smiled and set down the empty pan. "Carrots are in the icebox. Sugar's on the table." She pointed. "My son is convinced that if he provides enough sugar and carrots, one of the wandering jack mules will follow him home and take Thunder's place in harness."

"Don't the mules belong to anyone?"

"Of course they do. The prospectors and jack train

drivers know their animals, but they let them loose in town to graze. Saves on feed."

"Toby doesn't know about that?"

"I've told him, but he doesn't listen. Still, if a carrot or two keeps him busy, I'm sure the mules won't complain. Have you propped his leg between two pillows for the ride?"

"Yes, he showed me how. He was very cooperative."

"Toby's a friendly boy. He's just, well, energetic. Especially now that he's supposed to sit still. Good luck with him, Valentine. And with your search. Thank you, dear."

Vallie helped herself to sugar lumps and a carrot. As she and Toby began their trip up Bleeker Street, in her mind Mrs. Richardson's last words bounced about. *Dear. She called me dear,* Vallie thought. Something made her eyes sting. Just dust. She sniffed and patted Thunder's head. "Let's go find some hungry mules," she said.

Fortunately, that afternoon the jacks were too stubborn and independent to follow Toby home. Unfortunately, none of the rooming house ladies Vallie asked had heard of Papa. On the way back to Toby's house, she found the livery stables and scrawled a message for Bramblet Willis about her new job. When he got news of Papa, Vallie wanted to be sure he could find her right away.

At suppertime, Mr. Richardson agreed to employ

Valentine for as long as she could stay in Aspen while Toby's leg healed. After supper, she made a tiring trip to Papa's shack for her belongings and the kittens. With a big dog like Thunder in the house, Josie and Patsy weren't welcome there, but Mrs. Richardson said they could stay in the garden shed out back for a while.

For a while, Vallie thought as she trudged back into town with arms overflowing. Everything felt so temporary. *If* I find Papa, *when* Bramblet sends me back, *until* Toby's leg heals. There wasn't a person or thing Vallie could count on just now except herself and a couple of puny kittens. Not even Papa. And that hurt the most of all.

23

A Day at a Time

Toby liked to reenact every one of Vallie's adventures. On Tuesday, he pretended to be wicked Harold and snip off her braid while she feigned sleep. He pretended to be the ticket seller, and the sausage man in the depot, then sent Vallie off hunting a blue cap so that he could dress as a yard bull, and finally set the cap at a different angle to become the train conductor.

Mrs. Richardson seemed to think Vallie was wonderful, and even Toby's father smiled when Toby took the starring role in Omaha and made Vallie play the bully who frightened Joseph and Patrick.

Wednesday morning, Bramblet stopped by to report on his visit to the bank. "Your father has an account there," he began after meeting Mrs. Richardson and Toby. "A sizable account."

"What does that mean?" Vallie asked. "Is it good news or bad?"

"It means he has local connections at least. And several weeks ago, he withdrew a sum of money. The manager wouldn't tell me how much, but he indicated that Mr. Harper was planning a trip."

"A trip? So that's why he isn't here. But he will come back, if he has money in the bank, won't he?" *Please,* Vallie thought, crossing her fingers and wishing hard. *Papa just has to come back.*

"I think so. It's just that . . . What if he was going back to Pennsylvania to collect you?"

"Then I spoiled everything by coming out here, didn't I?" Vallie closed her eyes. "What a muddle. I was hoping . . ."

"Yes?" Bramblet looked at her seriously.

"That you'd wire Uncle Franklin and he'd let me stay here longer. More than just one week. The Richardsons understand that I might have to leave soon, but Toby needs help for a month until his leg mends, and he seems to like me and . . ."

Bramblet shook his head gently. "I'll try, Vallie, but don't count on it, all right? Shall we just take it a day at a time?"

"Please. I'm not in any kind of trouble. And they need me here."

"A day at a time, Vallie," Bramblet repeated. "Your uncle has the final say, you know. From his last wire I'd guess that wife of his is anxious to get you back under her protection. Bit of a fussbudget, is she?"

"More than a bit," Vallie sighed. "But still . . ."

He shook his head sadly. His face looked as solid and unchangeable as the hard rocks of the mountains. "Unless your uncle says otherwise, I'll come for you next Sunday after church. You'll want to be packed and ready."

As the week wore on, Vallie grew more and more discouraged. Bramblet brought no fresh news from the bank. And even though she knew Papa was probably on his trip, she kept asking at the rooming houses. For a man who'd lived here more than a year, it seemed as if he'd been invisible. Nobody knew him. The best Vallie could figure, he'd probably spent most of his time hiding out in the mountains, digging for that darned silver. *Where are you, Papa?*

By Saturday afternoon, she'd worked a full week. Toby had played all the way through her adventures several times, but unless her luck changed, the adventure would end on Sunday when Bramblet dragged her back to Pennsylvania. She didn't tell Toby, though. Foolish as it was, one part of her kept pretending she could stay.

Toby just plain kept pretending. His favorite role was that of the villain, Hiram Mosely, with Vallie switching from Bramblet Willis to herself armed with a plate of gravy in the form of a pie tin filled with dry spruce needles.

"Ouch! Oh, you've burned me!" Toby flung down the stick he pretended was a knife and brushed away the needles as if they were boiling hot.

"Catch him, boys, before he runs off," Vallie replied, taking one of Toby's thin arms as he sat on the back step. "We've got to haul him off to jail."

"Can't say as he'll do much running just now, but if you need help hauling this outlaw to jail . . ."

That voice . . . Vallie turned.

A man wearing a dark hat stood below the porch. He lifted his hat and smoothed back his hair in a gesture so familiar it brought tears to her eyes.

"Papa? Papa, is it really you?"

24

Tin Pan Dan

Papa bounded up the steps, pulled Vallie into a ferocious hug, lifted her off her feet and swung her around. "Valentine, heart of my heart!"

"Papa, you came! You came in time!"

Thunder barked and Toby began to shout. "Mama! Come quick! She's having another adventure. Hooray! Hooray!"

Mrs. Richardson rushed out the kitchen door and onto the back porch. "Whatever is going on out here? Toby, Thunder, hush now."

Papa still hadn't let go, and Vallie hugged him back as hard as she could. Finally everybody seemed to take a breath and it got quiet for a moment. Vallie's heart pumped so fast, she thought it might pop right out onto the porch.

"Mrs. Richardson, this is my father."

Papa bowed. "I'm Daniel Harper, ma'am."

"Ivy Richardson. And this is my son, Toby. If you'll give me a moment to get him inside, you two can speak in private."

"Oh, no, Mama, please. Let me stay. She's having an adventure and I'm in this one. Please, Mama."

Mrs. Richardson's cheeks grew red. "I'm sorry. He's a handful."

"That's all right, madam," Papa said. He settled himself and Vallie into the porch swing. "Toby can stay. He's no trouble. I've had an adventure or two myself he might like hearing about."

"Thank you. I'll bring you something cool, then. And Toby, you sit quiet and behave. No interrupting." Mrs. Richardson left, brought out glasses of iced tea and disappeared back into the house.

"Papa, where have you been? I've looked everywhere for you."

"It's a long story, sweetheart, but not nearly as exciting as yours, I'll wager. I didn't get written up in the newspaper."

Toby bounced on his seat. "She did. She had her story in the paper. My papa read it and I cut it out and pasted it in my scrapbook."

"You read about me too? Oh, Papa. I know I shouldn't have run away. It's just that I missed you so much and Harold was wicked, and . . ." Vallie buried her face in Papa's shoulder.

He patted her back and offered her his handkerchief. "Shall I tell you of my travels first, then, while you collect yourself?"

"Yes. Please."

"I've had some good luck, sweetheart. I found a rich vein of ore up on Shadow Mountain."

"I know. The kittens and I, we found it. We stayed there after . . . well, after they found out I was a girl and I lost my job in the café."

Papa shook his head. "Kittens too? You've had quite the time, haven't you? Are you sure you want to hear my ordinary little story?"

"Please, Papa, it can't have been ordinary. Where have you been?"

"Leadville. As I said, I found a rich vein of silver ore. I went to Leadville about two weeks ago with a train of jacks carrying my ore."

"I was in Leadville too, Papa. You might have walked right past me and not known it, because I was dressed as a boy."

"What a story, what a story." Toby thumped his thin chest. "Tomorrow I'm going to play the Leadville part. I'm going to play the papa."

Papa grinned at Toby and ruffled his red hair. Then he turned to Vallie. "What a trip, Valentine, my girl—from Pittsburgh to the Rockies, all alone." He hugged her again. "Thank the Lord you arrived safe and sound."

"Well, I did, Papa. Now tell me. Why were you gone so long in Leadville?"

"Yeah, why?" Toby echoed.

"I sold the load of ore I'd hauled. Once it proved to be high in silver, I arranged the sale of the mine too."

"The Valentine? You sold it?"

"I'm no miner, darling. Couldn't spend six days a week underground. And prospecting's a lonely business as well. I sold the Valentine Mine and the Annabelle too."

"Because?"

"I'm sick of mules. At heart, I'm still a schoolteacher. With the money from those mines, we'll have a good-sized nest egg, sweetheart. I can go back to teaching. While I was in Leadville, I sent you a long letter explaining all this. And money, for tickets, to bring you to Aspen."

"You were sending for me? While I was looking for you?"

"Better and better," Toby said. His eyes were fixed on Papa's face.

"Strange, isn't it? But once I saw the *Aspen Times* story, I knew I had to hightail it over the pass. That part about you disappearing from sight had me worried sick. I pushed hard and made the pass in two days."

"Two days? How did you find me here?"

"Stopped in at the Silver Dollar. The woman who

owns the place directed me to the Richardsons. Seems like everybody in town knows about the brave and fearless Valentine Harper." He smiled at Toby. "Your young fella with the broken leg has told anybody who cares to listen that you're staying at his house."

"That's right," Toby agreed loudly. "When we ride around town. Vallie asks for you and I tell everybody about my friend—the Silver Dollar Girl."

"Oh, Papa!" Vallie hugged him again.

"Now, Silver Dollar Girl. I've waited long enough. What made you leave your aunt Margaret's and how did you manage the trip?"

Vallie's story spilled out in bits and pieces as the ice melted in the iced tea and the porch swing drifted back and forth. Toby helped her tell his favorite parts. When she finally reached the end, Papa took her chin in his hand and looked her straight in the eye.

"I felt bad, Papa. Especially about Bridget. I know she worried . . ."

"Well, she'd be proud of you now, wouldn't she?"

"Proud?"

"You're taking care of this young boy the way she took care of you. I'd say that would make her heart swell."

What a funny idea, Vallie thought, smiling. But Papa was right. In taking care of Toby, she had become a bit like Bridget. "She might be proud, after she scolds me."

"Well, she'll probably scold me too," Papa said.

"For being gone too long. I hope she'll forgive us both. We'll send her a wire right away. Let her know you found me. I need to go to the bank anyway. Now that you're here we might as well start looking for a house."

"A house? Our own house? Here in Aspen?"

"Hooray!" Toby shouted again. "You can stay in town."

Papa chuckled. "I know the mine shack is real cozy, but I sold that with the mine. So unless you'd like to stay in my tent . . ."

"I'd like that," Toby said. "Course, a girl might be scared."

"I'm not scared of sleeping in a tent," Vallie said. "Might be fun every once in a while. But a real house would be nice too. I've been a stray long enough."

Papa's face turned serious. "I've been a stray myself, darling, climbing up this mountain and down that one with nobody but a mule to talk to. Didn't even answer to my own name part of the time. Tin Pan Dan, they called me. That's no kind of life. We need a home."

"How about across the street from us?" Toby asked. "Or next door?"

Papa stood up and grinned. "You think your young pal might excuse us long enough to walk to town, visit the bank and send a wire?"

Vallie hopped out of the swing. "How about it, Toby? Can I go off with my papa for a while?"

"I don't like this part." Toby frowned. "I guess you won't play with me anymore now since your papa came back."

She smiled. "I don't need a job. But I bet your mother still needs help. I'll come visit every day."

"For real?"

"Sure. We'll be friends because we want to, not just because I'm getting paid. That's better anyway, isn't it?" She punched his shoulder lightly.

Friends. Now she could make friends, just as she'd hoped. She knew Bo Reston would be pleased with her news. And she'd stop by the café and try to mend things with Nora Jensen. Now that Papa was back, surely the Jensens would forgive her.

Toby nodded and returned the punch. "When my leg heals, will you help me catch a jack?"

"I've got a better idea." Vallie lifted him in her arms and settled him on the cushions of the porch swing. "When your leg mends, we'll get Papa to take us out to visit Mr. Bramblet Willis. He's the detective."

"The one you saved?"

"I saved him, and he saved me too, in a way. We're even. But the thing is, Toby, he raises mules and horses. If you behave, you might get to ride one."

"How about you? Will you get to ride too? Will you behave?"

Vallie grinned and stepped out onto the front porch. "Guess I'd better, now that Papa's home."

Toby scowled. "Does that mean you're going to

turn into a sissy girl again, with ruffles and dolls? I don't like ruffles and dolls."

"I'm a girl, but I'm no sissy," Vallie said. "I'll keep my doll, but I'll keep my boots and my Levi trousers too. And I'll go easy on the ruffles, how's that?"

"That's my Silver Dollar Girl," Papa said. "Come on, Valentine, time's a-wasting." He waved to Toby and threw his arm around Vallie, and they started off to town.

Author's Note

The last decades of the 1800s have been called the Golden Age, the flowering of industrial America. As the nation turned from farming to industry, cities grew, transportation routes stretched across the land and machines increased the country's productivity.

In the eastern half of America, industrialists with good ideas and strong wills amassed huge fortunes in this age of opportunity. Bankers, men like Vallie's uncle Franklin, prospered. Most women, however, did not own businesses or work in banks; if they grew rich, it was through the efforts of their husbands or fathers. A girl like Valentine Harper would one day have married a man who would have supported her. Perhaps she'd have involved herself in charitable work, but only after she'd raised her children. America's industrial growth affected women of more modest means, however, by opening thousands of factory jobs and enticing girls and young women to leave small towns and work in cities.

The West was a different story. Instead of earning a fortune through business, people dreamed of digging their way to prosperity. The discovery of gold and silver in remote Western mountains lured men from all walks of life to head West, have adventures and start new lives. Some, like Daniel Harper, prospered. Many barely scraped by. But through their efforts, large tracts of Western land were settled.

Where these men lived, towns grew up, and married men sent for their wives and families to join them. Single men who decided to make a home in the West searched and even advertised back East for mail-order brides. And in the West, women were often expected to work alongside their men, as Nora Jensen does in the Silver Dollar Café.

Still, during the 1880s and 1890s, women, often a civilizing influence, were scarce in Western regions. Treasure-seeking adventurers tended to be more free-wheeling, less obedient to the rules of proper conduct, and without women, rowdy towns like Leadville earned bad reputations. From the very start, Aspen was unique. Fourteen wives and daughters joined the more than two hundred early male settlers, and even in its first year as a town, these women organized literary societies, musical evenings, schooling for children and churches. But Western women were not as tightly corseted as their Eastern sisters.

The 1880s were part of the Victorian era, named for the long reign of Victoria, queen of England. Victorians in America have a reputation for being formal and stuffy. Proper Eastern folk, like Vallie's aunt Margaret, avoided even polite references to parts of the body—a piano or a chair would have limbs, not legs, and one might consume a supper of baked chicken bosoms, not baked chicken breasts. But in the West, life was rougher, survival more difficult, and the niceties of Easterners gave way to a more casual, make-do style. It was hard to wear corsets and layers of petticoats while crossing the Rocky Mountains on a mule.

The fictional heroine of my story makes many of these discoveries herself as she travels from east to west. Vallie in Pennsylvania is a protected, cosseted, proper Victorian girl. In Aspen, when she pulls her skirts back on, leaves off all those petticoats and keeps her boots, Vallie is a thoroughly Western girl who has more freedom than the friends she left behind in Pennsylvania. The mountain sun will tan her skin, and the rough terrain will make her grow strong and sturdy, able to handle whatever challenges life brings.

Aspen, Colorado, exemplified the expansive Western spirit. First explored by white prospectors in 1879, it grew quickly and produced millions of dollars' worth of silver. The single largest silver nugget ever discovered was mined on Smuggler Mountain—it weighed more than a ton and had to be removed in three huge chunks. But Aspen, like other Western mining towns, depended on decisions made back East in Washington, D.C. In 1893, most of these boomtowns went bust when the government decided to use gold as the standard for currency instead of silver.

Some towns became permanent ghost towns. Others shrank and grew quiet for a time, until people discovered new sources of wealth in the mountains, such as skiing and other kinds of recreation. But even today, in high meadows and along craggy cliffs, tumbledown cabins and rusting machines bring to mind the early days. And in place names you can hear the echo of the silver miners: Tourtelotte Park, Silver Queen, the Mine Shaft, Silver Creek.

KATHERINE AYRES has been a lover of books since childhood. Born in Columbus, Ohio, she began inventing stories before she could write them. Her love of literature continued through her first career as a teacher and elementary school principal. She currently writes fiction for adults and children.

Katherine Ayres lives with her husband in Pittsburgh, where she skis, golfs, gardens, and quilts.